MAKING WAVES

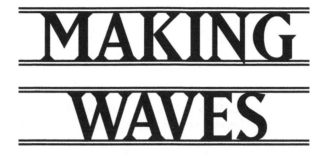

MAKING WAVES

BARBARA WILLIAMS

Dial Books for Young Readers

New York

Published by Dial Books for Young Readers
A division of Penguin Putnam Inc.
345 Hudson Street
New York, New York 10014
Copyright © 2000 by Barbara Williams
All rights reserved
Designed by Lily Malcom
Text set in Bembo
Printed in the U.S.A. on acid-free paper

1 3 5 7 9 10 8 6 4 2

Library of Congress Cataloging-in-Publication Data
Making waves/by Barbara Williams.
p. cm.
Sequel to: Titanic crossing.
Summary: Having survived the sinking of the Titanic in 1912,
twelve-year-old Emily moves to Baltimore, where she encounters child
labor, sweatshops, and the workers' struggle to form labor unions.
ISBN 0-8037-2515-9
[1. Social problems—Fiction. 2. Schools—Fiction.
3. Titanic (Steamship)—Fiction.] I. Title.
PZ7.W65587 Mak 2000
[Fic]—dc21   99-057832

The chart on page 159 is based on one from *Titanic: An Illustrated History*
by Don Lynch, illustrated by Ken Marschall, © 1992 by Madison Press
Books, and appears by permission.

The U.S. Senate hearings data on pages 206–207 is from *The Titanic Disaster
Hearings: The Official Transcripts of the 1912 Senate Investigation* © 1998
by Pocket Books, and appears by permission.

→ AUTHOR'S NOTE ←

Making Waves is a work of fiction based upon labor conditions in eastern United States factories between 1908 and 1916. Although the story doesn't record the events of specific lives, it was inspired by the heroism of Dorothy Jacobs Bellanca and other courageous men and women who risked blacklisting, beatings, and incarceration in their struggles to improve the soul-crushing environments that they and coworkers experienced. Bellanca, a native of Latvia, moved with her family to Baltimore when she was thirteen. Like Maggie Flanagan in *Making Waves,* she became the first president of the Hand Buttonhole Makers' union in Baltimore at the youthful age of fourteen.

The author is deeply indebted to the following people for their help with research: Alan Lessoff, Associate Professor of History, Texas A&M University, Corpus Christi, Texas; Roderick N. Ryon, Professor of History, Towson State University, Towson, Maryland; Mendy Gunter, Assistant

Manager, Maryland Department, Enoch Pratt Free Library, Baltimore, Maryland; Faith Fry, Sunsource researcher, *The Baltimore Sun,* Baltimore, Maryland.

CHAPTER ONE

Baltimore, Maryland
April 21, 1912

Dear Albert,

I hope you don't mind that I'm writing to you. I need to talk to someone who understands about the "Titanic."

Mama won't talk about it, and she has forbidden me to talk to Sarah or Robert for fear of upsetting them. They don't remember much anyway, though, because they slept on their lifeboat. Sarah was sick, and Robert was too little to know what was going on.

I hope your sister didn't catch Sarah's scarlet fever. Virginia certainly didn't sleep on our lifeboat. At first it was the yelling that kept her awake, but then it was the cold. After the boat drifted away from the people in the water who were yelling, Ginny kept crying about how cold she was and asking for your mother and your tutor. I cuddled her and told her stories, and that helped a little.

Here's what I need to talk to you about. I keep worrying that I might be going crazy. In the daytime I keep hearing the screams of the people in the icy water, and I think about them dying. Maybe your mother and uncle were nearby in the water and our boat could have rescued them. (The officer in charge wouldn't listen when a couple of us begged him to turn around.) At night I hate to go to sleep, because I have such terrible dreams that I wake up screaming. Do you have bad dreams? Please tell me I'm not the only one.

I'm afraid to start school tomorrow, but Mama says I have to. It hasn't been a week since the ship went down, but she says we have to get on with our lives. I'm scared to meet people who might think I'm crazy, but Mama gets mad when I say I want to stay home to mind Sarah and Robert. She says Sarah and Robert don't need me to stay with them because our landlady, Mrs. Lieberman, has agreed to keep an eye on things when I'm at school and Mama is at Brewer House.

Mama will be in charge of Brewer House when it opens in a couple of weeks. It is Baltimore's new settlement house, like Jane Addams's Hull House in Chicago. It's named after my father. (Imagine!) The plaque in the hall will read: "Franklin P. Brewer House, donated in honor of all Christian missionaries who died in the service of our Lord." Papa's rich cousin, Lucretia Brewer, gave the mansion and money to get everything started. (Papa never told me he had any rich relatives, but I guess he did.)

We came to Baltimore on the train Friday. Everything we owned was lost on the ship except for the nightclothes, shoes, and coats we were wearing when the "Titanic" sank. By tomorrow I'll have two dresses that a dressmaker is cutting down from things

that belonged to Cousin Lucretia. I already have a white fur muff
that Cousin Lucretia bought me as a surprise. It's very pretty, but
it doesn't make me want to go to school, which Mama thought
it would.

Sincerely yours,
Emily Brewer

P.S. A lady on our lifeboat was upset because, just before the
"Titanic" sank, she saw Col. J. J. Astor cutting up a lifejacket
with a knife to show his wife how it was made. Mama says being
rich isn't a sin, but I'm not so sure about Col. Astor. At least
Cousin Lucretia does good things with her money. Brewer House
will provide classes in health and child care for poor people,
mostly immigrants. Also a library and rooms for meetings.

P.P.S. You don't have to answer this letter if you don't want to,
but I hope you'll want to.

CHAPTER TWO

Standing beside her new teacher, Emily took a deep breath as she faced the other seventh graders. The high-ceilinged room was dimly lit and smelled of chalk.

"Attention, boys and girls," said Miss Cameron. "This is Emily Brewer, who is joining our class today. Do I have a volunteer to be her special friend this week and show her around the school?"

A round-faced girl in the front row yawned. Two rows behind her another girl stared at Emily before whispering to her neighbor, who studied her folded hands on her desk, trying to disguise a smile. Someone coughed nervously.

"Anyone?" Miss Cameron urged.

Emily shifted her weight from one foot to the other, feeling like a stray dog that nobody wants. She wished she hadn't decided to wear the brown silk dress today. Cut down from one of Cousin Lucretia's old Sunday outfits, it had seemed beautiful an hour ago. But now, among the cotton frocks or white shirtwaists and skirts the other girls were wearing, she felt conspicuous and dowdy. Gathering courage, Emily straightened her shoulders and stood taller.

Finally a frail, fair-haired girl sitting by the window raised her hand. "Irene Clayton!" The teacher removed the pince-nez glasses from her nose and used them to point to the girl. "Will you show Emily around today?"

"Yes, ma'am."

"You can take that empty seat next to Irene," Miss Cameron told Emily. For the first time Emily realized that the sturdy wooden desks with iron scrollwork on each side were bolted to the floor in pairs. As she raised one foot to start to the empty desk by Irene, a firm hand riveted her in place. "Not yet, Emily. We haven't said the Pledge yet. Pupils, please rise while Emily leads us in the Pledge."

The boys and girls shuffled to their feet and stared at Emily expectantly. She turned to Miss Cameron, her heart thumping. "The Pledge?"

"Yes. The Pledge of Allegiance to our flag. We always begin with the Pledge. You know it, don't you?"

"N-n-no, ma'am, I—"

Laughter exploded throughout the room as Emily's cheeks grew warm. So everyone thinks I'm an imbecile because I don't know some Pledge? she thought. I bet I'm the only person in the room who ever memorized poetry by Ovid. In Latin! I bet I'm the only one ever invited to recite from the *Tristia* for the British governor in Colombo. I bet . . .

Miss Cameron picked up a ruler and pounded her desk with it. *"Silence, boys and girls! Silence!"*

The teacher waited for the noise to stop and then spoke to Emily. "I'm sorry. I apologize." She turned to address the class. "Emily has been in Ceylon for three years, attending a mission school. Of course she wouldn't recite the Pledge of Allegiance to the American flag there. I'll lead the Pledge today."

The recitation began, Miss Cameron's singsongy voice one or two beats ahead of the students' monotone. Emily tried to listen so she would know how to lead the Pledge the next time that she was asked, but she couldn't understand the mushy-sounding words. Besides, she was so embarrassed standing in front of everyone that she couldn't think about anything but getting to her seat.

Relieved when the murmuring finally ended, Emily started toward the empty desk, but Miss Cameron grabbed her arm again. "Emily has had a very interesting life," she told the class. "We'll have to have her tell us about Ceylon when we study India in geography. And she's a cousin of Miss Lucretia Brewer. I'm sure you've all heard of Miss Brewer, who's building a neighborhood house about two miles from here to help the immigrants and poor people in that area."

The round-faced girl in the front row—the one who had yawned—rolled her eyes at the ceiling.

"The most interesting thing about Emily, though," continued Miss Cameron (after a breath so deep that it sent the pince-nez pinned to the shirtwaist over her ample bosom dancing on their gold chain), "is that she was on the *Titanic* when it sank last week."

"No fooling?" cried a boy in the rear.

Miss Cameron put the glasses back on her nose. "That's right. Why don't you tell us about it, Emily?"

Emily's heart flip-flopped. These weren't people she could talk to about the *Titanic*. She needed to talk to someone who would understand her feelings—someone who had been on the ship with her. Her mother was her first choice, of course, but Mama refused to discuss what had happened, or even listen when Emily tried to tell her about the wild dreams that awakened her every night in a cold sweat. "It isn't healthy to dwell on things you can't do anything about, Emily," Mama said. "You need to stay busy."

"Well?" the teacher prodded, smiling. Her teeth were large and even, like a horse's.

"How big was the swimming pool?" a boy yelled.

"Were the dishes really made of gold?"

"Is Mrs. Astor as pretty as her pictures?"

Even the girl in the front row was suddenly interested. She sat up straight. "Did you sit at the same table with Colonel Astor and his wife?"

Emily's fingernails dug into her flesh as she knotted her hands together. She wasn't really expected to answer questions like these, was she? Oh please, Miss Cameron, she thought, don't make me stand here like this. But Miss Cameron waited just as expectantly as the pupils, her thin lips slightly ajar.

"I—I didn't exactly meet Colonel and Mrs. Astor," Emily said. "I only saw them when we went to church on Sunday. They were traveling in first class, and I was in second."

"*Second class!*" The girl in the front row bobbed her head so violently that Emily could actually hear the crackling sound of her blue frock, starched rigid as cardboard, as her square shoulders wriggled. The girl leaned forward to eyeball Emily, crackling her dress again. "If you were only in second class, how come you were rescued and Colonel Astor wasn't?"

For some reason—although she hadn't actually seen him do it herself—Emily had an eerie vision of Colonel Astor using his pocketknife to cut open a lifejacket that belonged to someone else. She squinched her eyes shut and swallowed, fighting against the taste of breakfast oatmeal rising in her throat.

"Well?" the girl persisted. Emily opened her eyes to examine the girl's face. It was square, really—not round, as Emily had thought at first. And it seemed to rise not from a neck, the way most people's heads did, but directly from the girl's thick shoulders.

Emily squeezed her fingers tighter. "The officers told the men on the ship to wait until all the ladies and children were safely on board the boats."

"I should think that *someone* would have made room for Colonel Astor," the girl said.

"Well, I guess the officers decided—"

The girl's eyes were gray. And cold. Very cold. "Doesn't it make you feel guilty to know that you were rescued and Colonel Astor wasn't?"

"Louise!" the teacher hissed.

"But Colonel Astor was one of the richest men in the

world," Louise argued. "Everyone knows how important he was. Of all people, he should have been the one rescued."

"That's enough, Louise," said the teacher.

"And *she,*" Louise continued, not even looking at Emily but just shrugging in her direction as if she were dog excrement left on someone's lawn, "was only in second class!"

For an instant the teacher was too stunned to speak. At last she exhaled slowly, from somewhere deep inside that full bosom, her breath warm and coffee smelling against Emily's cheek. "No one needs to feel guilty for coming out of that terrible tragedy alive. Do they, Emily?"

"I—guess not," Emily whispered, not really agreeing with Miss Cameron but unable to squeeze out anything better to say. The lump in her throat was the size of a cantaloupe, and she knew she couldn't say more without bursting into tears. Instead, she looked down at the tops of her scuffed black shoes, wondering if there would ever be a time when she felt talkative and confident again, the way she had always been before the ship sank.

"You may take your seat, Emily."

The words sounded hollow, far away.

"I said you may take your seat."

"Uh—yes, ma'am."

Sniffing, she stumbled along the graying wooden floor-boards to the empty desk. She needed a handkerchief. Why hadn't Cousin Lucretia bought her one instead of a useless fur muff? Would anyone notice if she wiped her nose on her sleeve? Of course they would. Didn't they have anything else to stare at?

"Please turn to chapter twelve in your science books, boys and girls."

Emily sank to the curving wood seat attached to the oak desk. Around the room other pupils were opening books, but there were no books on her desk.

"Page one sixty-eight, Emily," said Miss Cameron in a patronizing tone.

Emily stared at her desktop—at the round hole in the upper right-hand corner (for a bottle of ink?); at the long horizontal groove in the back and center (for a pencil?); at the scratches and carved initials in the surface. Where was the book she was supposed to open? She couldn't think.

"You'll find your science book inside your desk," Miss Cameron said patiently.

Emily ducked her head. Resting on a shelf beneath her desktop were three books, all protected by makeshift covers of heavy brown paper. With her head down she felt invisible enough to wipe her nose with the back of her hand. Then she quickly seized one of the books before sitting up straight again.

"Not that one!" Her seatmate reached over to snatch the book from Emily's hands. Irene's voice was deep for someone so seemingly frail. She returned the book to the shelf in Emily's desk and grabbed another. "This one! Page one sixty-eight!"

"Thank you," Emily murmured thickly as she flipped the pages back and forth. Where was page 168? Why was her vision so fuzzy? Why couldn't she do a simple task like finding the right page? Oh, there it was. She exhaled a small sigh of relief.

"Do you have the place now?" the teacher asked in her too-patient tone.

"Yes, ma'am." Oh please, Emily thought, don't treat me like a five-year-old. Don't make everyone stare at me.

Miss Cameron took a handkerchief from a skirt pocket to polish her glasses. "I'm going out into the hall for a minute. I'd like all of you to read chapter twelve silently, and I'll give you a quiz on it when I get back. Edward, you act as room monitor and take down the names of any pupils causing a disturbance. Louise, I'd like to see you out in the hall, please."

At Emily's side Irene gasped out loud. She poked Emily with an elbow. "Now you'll catch it," she whispered.

"From Miss Cameron?"

"From Louise."

"Why? What did I do?"

"You got her into trouble with the teacher," Irene whispered.

"What can she do to me?"

"Emily," said Miss Cameron in her honeyed voice, "I don't know how things were in Ceylon, but we don't talk in this class."

Once more all the other pupils turned to stare at the new girl. Silence hung in the room like black smoke.

Through blurry eyes Emily looked at her science book in its makeshift brown paper cover, pretending a vital interest in chapter twelve's explanation of the solar system.

CHAPTER THREE

Da-clang! Da-clang! Da-clang! Someone out in the hall was ringing a bell.

Quizzical, Emily turned toward Irene. "What's that?"

"Put your book in your desk and get your coat."

At the rear of the room girls were already removing their coats from hooks along the wall. Several boys, with only one arm in a coat sleeve, were rushing to line up by the door.

"What's going on?" Emily wanted to know.

"Recess," Irene explained as she stood to walk down the aisle.

Now that she was no longer pretending to read her science book, Emily studied her "volunteer" helper. Irene Clayton was a tall, blond girl with eyebrows so pale they were barely visible, and skinny arms that seemed all bones, and sharp elbows. From one of the classroom hooks she snatched an old coat that was several sizes too small and pushed the four mismatched buttons through the holes. Her birdlike hands hung well beyond the ends of the sleeves.

Emily reached for her own coat, which was no better. For modesty's sake she had worn it over her nightclothes day and night for a week, not merely on the *Titanic's* lifeboat, but all the way to New York on the *Carpathia*. It stank of brine and cigar smoke. And the sweat of raw fear.

Ready for the April elements, Emily and Irene joined the line at the side of the room and waited for the teacher's signal to leave. When all the stragglers were in line, Miss Cameron nodded for the pupils to begin their solemn procession through the hall. Boys and girls from other classes were already marching through the poorly lit corridor in single-file rows—step, step, step, step—as regimented as the British soldiers in Colombo. Along the hall they paraded. Down the stairs to the first floor. Through the outside door of the school. Down the seven steps to the concrete playground. There, at last, the ranks splintered like glass, girls tittering as they hurried to play jump rope or hopscotch, boys pumping their arms and shouting as they sped to the baseball diamond or to draw rings in the dirt for games of marbles.

Emily raced behind Irene and tugged at her coat sleeve. "What can Louise do to me?"

Irene spun around, looking impatient. "Plenty. I guess I should know. I got her into trouble last year."

Emily tried to remember what she and Louise had said to each other about Colonel Astor and the *Titanic*. "I didn't do anything. If Louise is in trouble with Miss Cameron, she did it herself."

"That's what I thought last year. But Louise gets even with people who cross her. She bullies people, even the boys, just because she's the richest girl in the school. Her father is . . . *Joseph Kezerian!*" Irene sucked in her cheeks, waiting for Emily to absorb that amazing revelation.

"Who's Joseph Kezerian?"

"You've never heard of Joseph Kezerian?"

Emily shook her head. "No."

"Kezerian's Fruit and Vegetable Cannery?"

Emily shook her head again.

"He owns it. Seaside Fish Cannery too. The two biggest canneries in Baltimore. In Maryland, even. My mother works at the fruit-and-vegetable place, so Louise thinks that gives her the right to bully me. And everyone else in the school."

Emily had never met a bully. The young people she had known in Ceylon were gentle and kind, but Emily had read stories about bullies and street toughs in America. She had a terrifying vision of provoking broad-shouldered Louise Kezerian into a fistfight.

"Maybe she's just lonely. Maybe she means well—"

"Means well?" Irene scoffed at the idea. "She's a bully. The girls stay out of her way, but the boys let her play baseball with them sometimes. She can't run the bases worth spit, but that doesn't matter 'cause she usually hits a home run. I've never hit a home run, have you?"

"I've never played baseball," Emily admitted. "We didn't do that in Ceylon. We just—"

"I wish she'd move to Roland Park, don't you?"

"What's Roland Park?" Emily asked.

"You've never heard of Roland Park? That's where all the hoity-toity people live. The houses are as big as a dozen row houses—no kidding—and every one of them has its own yard. With grass! There's even a country club and golf course."

Emily nodded, remembering the huge governor's palace in Colombo. "In Ceylon—"

"Well, I wish she'd move there. We don't need her in our school, lording it over everybody else. If rich people can't be nice to the rest of us, they should go off by themselves. Don't you think so?"

Actually, Emily didn't think so. She had looked forward to coming back to America, which Papa had told her so much about. It was democratic, he had said, a melting pot. Everybody was equal here, he insisted, but Emily was beginning to suspect that wasn't true. It certainly hadn't been true on the *Titanic*. She had been shocked to discover how people were treated on the ship, with first-class passengers given special privileges, even at church, and third-class passengers left below in steerage when the *Titanic* hit the iceberg. She shuddered.

"Louise keeps saying she's going to move to Roland Park, but she never does. I bet I know why. Shall I tell you?"

Emily shrugged. She was sure Irene would tell her whether she wanted to hear or not.

"I'll bet her father was blackballed at that ritzy Roland Park country club. Rich people don't like just anybody, you know, even other rich people. Louise will get you back if you cross her, especially if you do it in April and May.

You have to be nice to her then or she'll get even with you, the way she did to me last year."

"You still haven't told me what happened last year."

"Wel-l-l," Irene began, drawing out the word, "Louise brought a peashooter to school. We aren't allowed to bring them because the little children—first and second graders—cry when people shoot them."

"What are peashooters?"

"You've never seen a peashooter? They're tubes, sort of like drinking straws, only made of wood. Kids put dried peas and beans in them and blow as hard as they can. The peas are hard, almost like rocks, and they sometimes hurt. It's even worse when people keep the peas in their mouths and get them all slobbery."

Emily winced. She didn't blame little children for not wanting to be shot with someone's slobber. "So did Louise shoot a first grader?"

"No. She shot me. Right in the eye. It hurt something awful, and for about an hour I couldn't see out of that eye. I thought I was going blind."

"So you told the teacher?" Emily asked.

"No. The principal. Mrs. Hiskey sent a note home to Louise's parents saying she wanted to see them at school. *On the first day of May!*"

"What's so important about May?"

"Her birthday is June eighth. She'd already invited me to her party, but after I tattled on her, she told me I couldn't come."

Relief flooded over Emily like a refreshing summer

shower. She had been having terrible visions of a fistfight with the school bully, but the thing Irene was talking about was only a birthday party.

"Oh, is that all?" said Emily.

"It ruined my life is all."

"I don't see how not going to a birthday party could ruin anyone's life."

"You will when you're not invited this year. Louise has the best birthday parties in the whole world. Two years ago her father rented a trolley car, a whole trolley car just for Louise's party. We drove all over Baltimore, singing and waving to the people outside, and eating hot dogs, and drinking sarsaparilla. We just about drove the motor-man crazy. The trolley left the overhead wire *three times,* and we made fun of him when he had to put on his gloves and go out back to set the wheel on the track again."

Unable to think of anything to say, Emily merely nodded.

"Last year her father rented a private boat and took everyone out on Chesapeake Bay," Irene went on. "For a whole afternoon. It was all anyone could talk about all summer long. But I wasn't invited, so I just sat around like a lump of used chewing gum while everyone raved and raved about how much fun they'd had on the boat."

Emily stiffened.

"And this year Louise's party is going to be even better," Irene continued. "She promised. She hasn't told us what it will be, but she's been saying for weeks that it will be even better than a private boat ride. So you'd better try to make things up with her if you want to be invited this year."

"I hope she doesn't ask me," Emily said softly.

"You don't want to go to her party?"

The thought of a boat ride, even a pleasant ride around Chesapeake Bay, had brought back the terrifying images. Inside Emily's head the noise had returned too—the screams of people in the icy Atlantic, begging to be saved.

"No."

"Yes, you do. *Everyone* wants to go to Louise's parties."

Emily wasn't listening. She was thinking about how cold she'd been when she was tending Albert Trask's little sister in the *Titanic* lifeboat. She pulled her coat around her tighter.

Someone punched her shoulder. Was it Virginia Trask? No, of course not. The two of them had been rescued. Emily was on the playground of her new school in Baltimore.

Louise Kezerian grabbed Emily's arm. "Hey! I'm talking to you."

"Oh . . . sorry," said Emily.

"Miss Cameron is watching us, so look at me and smile." Louise glared at Emily with cold, gray eyes.

"Uh—" Emily stammered.

"She told me I had to apologize to you. So that's what I'm doing." With that, Louise spun around and hunched toward the spot where a group of boys was playing marbles.

"See what I mean?" whispered Irene. "See how she treats people who cross her? But her parties are wonderful, so be nice to her."

"Wait!" Emily ran after Louise.

"What do you want? I apologized, didn't I?"

"But—you didn't need to," Emily explained. "I mean, you were right. I should feel guilty—about the *Titanic*."

Louise scowled. "I know why you're saying that. I heard what Irene said to you. You just want to be invited to my party."

"No. No, I don't."

"Yes, you do. Everyone does."

"I'm not like everyone. I mean, I don't care about your party. I—I had no right to be saved on one of the *Titanic* lifeboats when—" Her voice broke. She was thinking not only about Colonel Astor, but also about Albert Trask's mother and uncle, who had died. And about the hundreds of third-class passengers trapped in the bowels of the ship. She had to take a deep breath before she could push out the rest of her sentence. "When more important people weren't."

The scowl on Louise's face seemed to fade a little.

"Anyway," Emily added, "I want you to know I'm sorry if I got you in trouble with Miss Cameron."

Louise stared at Emily for a moment, a hint of a smile on her lips, before speaking. "That's okay. She doesn't scare me."

Emily watched as Louise hurried off toward the boys. She turned toward Irene. "I'd like to go to the bathroom before we have to go back to class. Will you show me where it is?"

"Yes, but don't use the soap in there. It will eat your skin off."

CHAPTER FOUR

A streak of light cut through the classroom the next day as a boom of thunder rattled the four windowpanes in the wall.

"Ooh! That was close!" Irene whispered to Emily as she hugged herself into a ball. "I hate thunderstorms, don't you?"

Emily nodded, even though she didn't mind rain too much. Compared to the biting cold and blackness she had experienced on the lifeboat a week ago, a few flashes of lightning were almost pleasant. But she wished the electric lights would come back on. When the thunder shook the windows, the room darkened from a sallow yellow to a greenish gray.

Miss Cameron walked to the opposite side of the room and fiddled with the switch, but the overhead lights didn't come back on again. "I'm afraid the lightning hit the power line," she said at last. "It's going to be difficult to read in here without electricity. And we can't very well go outside for physical education," she added as huge raindrops pelted the windows like gravel. Then, her lips stitched into a knot, she stood at the side of the room, thinking.

"Let's have a dancing lesson," suggested Louise Kezerian.

Emily sat up straight, wondering if she had heard correctly. Home run–hitting Louise Kezerian was exactly the last person Emily would expect to suggest a dancing lesson. She certainly didn't look like a ballerina. What kind of dancing did she have in mind? Emily felt sure that anyone who had trouble running around the diamond in a game of grade-school baseball couldn't do any high-stepping folk dances—or the intricate temple dances performed by the ruffled and bangled worshipers in Ceylon.

Whatever kind of dancing Miss Cameron taught the class, Emily hoped the teacher wouldn't make her do it. It was hard to think about anything but the *Titanic*. She wondered if she could raise her hand and ask to be excused from dancing. But what excuse could she give? Would the teacher understand that Emily didn't feel like dancing? Would anyone understand that dancing seemed disrespectful for her to be doing so soon after witnessing all those horrible deaths?

In the front of the class Miss Cameron beamed at Louise. "That's a splendid idea. While the power is off, we can teach Emily the waltz that the rest of you have been learning."

Emily's heart sank. Of course Miss Cameron wouldn't excuse her from dancing.

"Who would like to play the piano today?" the teacher asked her class.

Irene Clayton shot both hands toward the ceiling like

twin cannonballs, and suddenly Louise's request for a dancing lesson made sense to Emily. Louise didn't want to dance, Emily decided; she wanted to play the piano. But Louise didn't raise her hand the way most of the other girls were doing. That struck Emily as strange. If Louise's father was really as rich as Irene had told her, she would be the most likely girl in this class to have a piano in her home and to have taken music lessons.

On the other hand, Irene Clayton seemed desperate to accompany the dancers as she motioned frantically to get the teacher's attention.

Touching Irene's shoulder, Emily spoke softly. "Can you play the piano?"

Irene answered without looking at her. "Sure. It's easy."

"Have you taken lessons?"

"No, but I've watched Miss Cameron. I can do it."

Emily's admiration for her seatmate suddenly soared. Emily herself couldn't play the piano, although she had watched Papa's British friend Mr. Warwick do it scores of times in Ceylon. He owned a piano and sometimes allowed Emily and Sarah to play "Chopsticks" on it when they went to visit.

"Mmm," said Miss Cameron as she studied the room for volunteers.

"Miss Cameron! Miss Cameron!" Irene whispered huskily to get the teacher's attention. Her skinny arms were whipping the air.

Unable to ignore Emily's seatmate, the teacher removed her pince-nez and pointed with them. "Irene, you may be our accompanist today. All right, boys and girls, please line up by the front door and wait for the signal to march to the auditorium."

Irene grinned in Emily's direction. "Playing the piano is so much fun! And now I won't have to be Louise's partner."

As Louise lumbered toward the queue that was forming at the side of the room, Irene sidled up to her. "I'm sorry I can't be your partner today. It's fun to dance with you, but Miss Cameron needs me to play the piano."

Louise shrugged as Emily stared in puzzlement from her to Irene. Did all the girls—maybe some of the boys too—treat Louise so shabbily? Saying one thing to her face and another behind her back? Pretending to be her friend for five or six weeks every year just so she would invite them to her famous birthday parties? No wonder Louise acted like an obnoxious bully in return. Anyone would.

After marching single file to the auditorium, directly below their seventh-grade classroom, the boys and girls seemed to know they were supposed to form separate lines facing each other. Irene headed toward the piano, so Emily found a place in the girls' line.

"No, no," said the teacher as she seized Emily by the shoulders and pushed her between Louise and another girl who was standing next to her. "We line up according to height. You stand here by Louise." She stood back to survey the lines. "There. That's perfect."

It seemed that Miss Cameron was trying to pair each girl with a boy who was the same height or a little taller, but that wasn't possible among these pupils. Emily had heard that girls reached their adult height sooner than boys, but she had never been in a situation before where that fact was so obvious. Many of these seventh-grade girls were taller than the boys, and Louise, who was the tallest pupil in the room, had broader shoulders, besides. There were also more girls than boys, three more if you counted Irene, who was opening the lid of the piano bench. That left Louise and Emily as the two tallest remaining girls, the ones who would probably have to dance together.

Miss Cameron had joined Irene at the piano, and together they were examining the labels on some rectangular boxes they had pulled from the piano bench. Selecting one of the boxes, Miss Cameron removed a roll of paper from it and put the box back into the bench. After sliding to either side a pair of ornate doors on the upright part of the piano, she set the roll of paper on a rod toward the top of the exposed area and pulled down one edge of the paper to attach it to a hook on a rod below. Leaving the doors open, she struck a chord on the piano and addressed the pupils.

"Attention, boys and girls! Attention! Emily hasn't had social dancing with our class before, so I want you to show her what ladies and gentlemen you are when you dance. We'll begin dancing to 'On the Beautiful Blue Danube.' Emily, have you ever done the waltz?"

"No, ma'am," she said. And I don't want to, she thought.

"Uh—" The teacher looked around the room. "Wilson, will you please explain how it's done?"

Wilson mumbled something to the tops of his shoes that Emily couldn't understand.

"Speak up, Wilson," ordered the teacher. "Say it so Emily can understand you."

"One-two-close," he said.

"That's right. One-two-close, one-two-close. It's the easiest dance step, so it's a good one for learning social dancing. Emily, you can dance with Louise for now. She's taller, so she'll be the boy. The boy holds the girl's right hand in his left. He puts his right arm around her waist, and he puts her left hand on his shoulder. Then he guides her around the floor, dancing one-two-close, one-two-close. Do you understand, Emily?"

"I think so, ma'am," she said aloud, but silently she thought, Oh, please don't make me.

"All right, Irene. You may begin the music."

Already seated on the piano bench, Irene began pumping her feet back and forth on two large pedals near the floor as the roll of paper wound down and around to reveal strange-looking holes. Without her touching any of them, the keys of the piano magically went down and back up again as beautiful music—as wonderful as the tunes Mr. Warwick had played in Ceylon—poured forth from the instrument.

Louise held out her left hand for Emily to take. "I guess we have to dance together. Come on."

Although neither girl was especially graceful, the waltz proved to be as easy as Miss Cameron had said, and Emily decided she might as well try to enjoy herself. She looked at her partner. "This isn't too bad. I thought dancing would be harder."

No sooner had she spoken than Louise stepped on her foot. "Sorry," Emily said. "I guess I haven't caught on very well yet."

Louise didn't answer.

"Don't you like dancing?"

"Sometimes."

"You're the one who suggested it," Emily reminded her.

"I suppose."

"Why?"

"None of your business."

Emily caught her breath. "Oh. Sorry."

They danced silently for a few minutes. "You remind me of a boy I know," Emily said at last.

"Someone you love to dance with, I'll bet," Louise said sarcastically.

"I haven't ever danced with him. He probably hasn't ever tried it either. But that isn't the reason you remind me of him."

Louise didn't respond.

"Would you like to know why?"

"Not especially."

"Well, I'm going to tell you anyway. He wasn't very nice to me when we first met. He pretended he didn't like me. But he didn't know me well enough to *not* like me, so I didn't worry about the sarcastic things he said. I knew he was just lonely."

"You think I'm lonely?"

"Mmm-hmm." Even though she hadn't felt much like making small talk since the sinking, Emily was used to telling people what she thought, and she wasn't going to let Louise's reputation as a bully stop her.

"All right, smart aleck, exactly what makes you think so?" Louise asked.

"You didn't eat lunch with anyone yesterday. And you walked home alone from school. I think you don't have any friends."

"I don't need friends."

"Yes, you do. Everyone does."

"Gee whiz. How was I lucky enough to get a nonstop philosopher for a dance partner? Well, do us both a favor and save all your brilliant theories for your boyfriend. I'm sick of listening to you."

"See, that's what I mean. You're exactly like Albert. He pretended he didn't want to talk to me either at first. But I could tell he was really lonely."

"Poor Albert!"

"Yes, poor Albert. He was just too shy to say the things he was really thinking. He finally warmed up, though, and we became good friends. I think you're like that. You and I could be friends."

"Hmm."

"You're not the only person in this school who had to walk home alone yesterday. I did too. I don't have any friends here either."

"How about Irene Clayton?" Louise made a face, as if Irene's name tasted bad.

"She talks to me because the teacher said she has to, but she isn't exactly a friend," Emily explained. "Besides, I can't walk home with her. She lives in the other direction. I wish Albert lived in Baltimore."

"Is he someone you knew in Ceylon—the place where Miss Cameron said you came from?" Louise's tone had lost its edge.

"No. I met him on the ship coming to America. On the *Titanic*. He lives in Virginia."

"Virginia isn't very far away."

"It is when my papa is dead and my mama doesn't own a motorcar." Emily saw no point in mentioning Cousin Lucretia's Packard, because Papa's cousin didn't use her fancy motorcar for frivolous things. Emily was certain that the serious-minded Miss Brewer, who was always worrying about the "less fortunate" and donating her money to charities, could never be persuaded to drive all the way to Virginia just to visit a boy whom Emily had known for such a short time. "Mama doesn't even have a carriage," she added.

"How about his father? Does his father own an automobile?"

"Albert is an orphan. His father died nearly a year ago, and his mother—his mother died on the *Titanic*."

"Oh . . . " Louise didn't seem to know what to say.

"Albert lives with his grandmother now. She probably has an automobile. I don't know for sure. But I don't imagine she lets Albert drive it. At least not this far."

"There's always the train," Louise suggested. "Why don't you ask him to come visit you on the train?"

"I've thought about that, but our house is in quarantine right now. I've already had scarlet fever, but my little sister caught it from someone on the tramp steamer we took around the Cape of Good Hope. In fact, she probably gave it to Albert's sister, Ginny, on our rescue ship after the *Titanic* sank, because she was in our cabin. Anyway, I think Albert might not want to leave Ginny so soon after their mother's death."

"Maybe they could both come."

"Maybe. But I'd kind of like to see Albert alone. Ginny always takes over when she's around."

"You're sweet on him, aren't you?"

"Of course not!"

"Yes, you are."

Emily hoped her cheeks weren't as red as they felt. "I need a good enough reason to make him want to come. What would you tell him if you were me?"

"I'd tell him I was sweet on him and wanted him to come see me."

Emily was aghast. "You wouldn't!"

"Well, maybe not." Louise was silent for a while as they danced, stumbling over each other's feet a couple of times. "Royal Ludlow probably thinks I'm sweet on him just because I always try to get to him first when we have girls' choice for dancing. Other girls beat me sometimes. Everyone wants to dance with him. He's the best dancer in our class. The best in the whole school."

Emily grinned as the light finally dawned. "That's why you wanted to have dancing class today, so you could dance with him! You're sweet on him."

"Don't be dumb."

"Now *you're* blushing. You're sweet on Royal Ludlow."

"Lower your voice, would you? Anyhow, there wasn't anything else we could do. It was too dark to read." Again Louise was briefly silent before sharing her intimate thoughts. "Royal never chooses me when it's boys' choice, but I think he's just shy, like your friend Albert. I think Royal must like me a little. I'm always the first girl he chooses when he's the captain of the baseball team, but the only time we dance together is when it's girls' choice. Most of the time Miss Cameron makes me dance with Irene Clayton. You want to know something? Irene is a two-face. She didn't mean it when she said she was sorry we wouldn't be dancing together today, but that's all right because I didn't want to dance with her either."

Emily couldn't help feeling sorry for Louise.

The realization that Louise Kezerian—tough-acting Louise—was sweet on a boy made her seem even more vulnerable and lonely than Emily had suspected.

"Why don't we walk home from school together?" Emily said. "We walk in the same direction."

"Okay," Louise said with a shrug, but her eyes gave her pleasure away. "And I'll tell you something you can say to Albert that will make him want to come to Baltimore."

"Really? That's wonderful!"

The lights in the school corridor suddenly came on just as the music of the "Blue Danube" waltz ended. As she had done before, Miss Cameron struck a chord on the piano to get everyone's attention.

"It's getting late, boys and girls, and we need to get back to our lesson. I'll ask Irene to play one more waltz. Let's make it boys' choice, shall we?"

"Oh darn," Louise mumbled.

"Maybe he'll ask you. He's looking right this way," Emily said.

Miss Cameron cleared her throat. "I want all of you to show Emily what gracious manners we use when we choose our partners." She turned to face Emily as she explained.

"The gentleman always walks over to the lady and says, 'Would you please care to dance?' and the lady replies, 'I would be happy to.' And when the dance is over, they both thank each other for a lovely time. All right, gentlemen, you can choose your partners while I put a new roll of music in the piano."

Emily nudged Louise. "Don't look now, but Royal Ludlow is coming straight over. You don't have to dance with me anymore."

"Are you sure?"

Before Emily could answer, Royal had sauntered toward Emily, not Louise. He punched her arm, his face so close to hers that she took an involuntary step backward. "Hey, do you want to dance?" he asked.

"Uh—" Emily stammered. She didn't want to be rude, but she wished there were something she could say to make Royal choose Louise instead.

"Well, do you want to or don't you?" he asked. "Other girls do if you don't."

Emily wasn't quite sure what he meant by that remark. Was he boasting or trying to be funny? She looked toward Louise for some signal, but Louise, her eyes cast downward, was already heading toward the chairs at the side of the room. "Yes, of course. I would be happy to," Emily told him.

With a smug expression Royal took her firmly in his arms, and she watched over his shoulder, feeling uncomfortable as Louise sat alone at the side of the room. Then something unpredictable happened. As the music began, Emily felt as graceful as a bird in Royal's arms as he guided her across the room. Even more amazing was the way he moved his feet to the music—lightly, gracefully, rhythmically. Louise was right. Royal Ludlow—ordinary-looking Royal Ludlow, who sat across the aisle from her in class—was an incredible dancer. She wasn't even tempted to talk. The experience of moving her body to the music was too exhilarating.

When the dance was over, she looked toward him with a smile, trying unsuccessfully to withdraw her hand. "Thank you for a nice dance."

Shouldn't he let go of her hand now? she wondered. Shouldn't he be thanking her for the dance too? Maybe he didn't think she was a very good dancer, but she hadn't stumbled against his feet the way she did when she danced with Louise. She felt uncomfortable standing there, where everyone could see them holding hands. No one else was holding hands. She couldn't think of anything to say. Was Louise watching?

"Um—Louise told me what a good waltzer you are," Emily stammered.

"The waltz is for old fogies like Miss Cameron. Can you do the Turkey Trot?"

"No. I never did any kind of dancing in Ceylon. Once I watched the temple dancers—"

"The Turkey Trot is fun. I'll teach you." He let go of her hand and began to whistle, holding his shoulders straight as his feet moved skillfully to the lively rhythm. Royal wasn't a bit ordinary-looking when he danced. He was more graceful than the temple dancers in Ceylon. Her heart pounded as she watched him.

There was something familiar about the dance he was doing. Where had she seen that dance and heard that tune before?

And then she remembered. It was on the boat deck of the *Titanic*. The officers were shouting as they tried to load the people into the boats, but no one believed the ship was really sinking because the lights were still on and the orchestra was playing that happy-sounding music. People were dancing.

Emily shuddered and covered her eyes with her hands.

"Hey! What's the matter?" Royal asked.

She dropped her hands from her face to wring them instead. "Nothing."

"Is my singing that bad?" he joked.

"No. Of course not. It's that song. I've heard it before."

"Well I should hope so. Everyone has heard the Turkey Trot music, even in Ceylon, I'll bet. Come on, I'll teach you the steps." He took her hand.

"No. I—I can't"

"Of course you can, if you try."

"Not today. Please."

"You must think I'm not a good enough dancer to teach you."

"No, that isn't it. You're a wonderful dancer," Emily said. "Louise told me she loves to dance with you."

Royal said nothing. He just stared at her with deep-set eyes that were almost obscured by the thick brows above them.

At last he gave her hand a squeeze, an embarrassingly affectionate squeeze. "Louise should stick to baseball."

With that, Royal let go of her and walked off to line up with the other pupils at the side of the room.

Back in the classroom Emily felt Royal looking at her from across the aisle, but she was too confused to return his gaze. What had he meant by squeezing her hand that way? Should she tell Louise about it? No, of course not.

Suddenly, as Emily watched from her side of the aisle, Royal snatched a live bug from the floor, set it on his desktop, and hunkered down so low that his heavy eyebrows were only a few inches away. Then slowly he dismembered the insect, one leg and one wing at a time. Oooh! she thought. How horrible. What kind of a person would enjoy doing a thing like that—deliberately causing pain to another creature with his bare hands?

She looked down at her own hands, the one she had rested on Royal's shoulder and the one he had squeezed. She felt terrible about what she had done today. What would Albert think if he knew she had danced with a boy—with not just any boy, but that horrid Royal Ludlow—so soon after Albert's mother and uncle and fifteen hundred other people had died screaming in the water? She could hardly wait for recess, when she could go to the girls' bathroom and scrub Royal's touch from her skin, scrub her hands raw with the foul-smelling lye soap that the janitor kept in there.

CHAPTER FIVE

McLean, Virginia
April 23, 1912

Hello, Emily,

No, you're not crazy. At least I hope not. Did you know I also witnessed the event with Col. J. J. Astor? And I have a bad dream too; the same one over and over. I keep seeing hundreds of people desperate to break a locked gate in the "Titanic's" steerage. In my dream I know that Mother has gone to steerage to find a lady she needs to talk to, and I see her face and Uncle Claybourne's among the others. When the gate finally opens, they push and yell in panic as they try to climb eleven flights of stairs to the boat deck. Suddenly I wake up and realize that I am the one who is yelling. Then I lie in the dark, worrying about what I could have done to save Mother and Uncle Claybourne.

It's too late to save them, but there must be something I can do to keep a terrible accident like that from ever happening again.

Every day I read the newspaper about the hearings that Senator William Alden Smith is holding about the "Titanic" in Washington. If I still lived in Washington, I would go to the Capitol. Someone needs to tell him and the other Senators about three very serious problems:

1. *There weren't enough lifeboats for all the passengers and crew on board the ship.*
2. *Captain Edward J. Smith never held a lifeboat drill so people would know where they were supposed to go in an emergency.*
3. *Passengers in third class were kept from getting to the boat deck on time.*

Do you think the witnesses will report all these things?

Thanks for writing to me. I know what you mean about not having anyone to talk to. I had hoped things would be different when I got back to America, but they're not. All my old friends live in Washington, not here in the country. Grandmother spends a lot of time in her bedroom. I'm not sure what she does in there, but I think she's crying about Uncle Claybourne. She comes out with her face all puffy and red.

Virginia used to talk a lot (I guess you remember that!), but right now she has a sore throat and doesn't say anything. Yes, she caught Sarah's scarlet fever, but I

*probably won't. Grandmother thinks I had it when
I was little.*

*The doctor comes every day to "paint" Ginny's throat.
He uses a long stick with cotton on the end that he sticks in
nasty-tasting red medicine. Ginny tries to cover her mouth
when he goes into her room. Then she makes terrible faces
when he's through. I read to her, but she's too sick to play
games or anything. Maybe I'll teach her checkers or
pachisi when she starts feeling better.*

*I hope you'll write again soon. I mean, if you feel like it.
Tell your mother and Sarah and Robert hello from*

> *Your friend,*
> *Albert Trask*

*P.S. Do you think it would help if I wrote a letter to
Senator Smith? I don't have his address, but maybe I could
just say in care of the U.S. Capitol.*

CHAPTER SIX

Baltimore, Maryland
April 26, 1912

Dear Albert,

I was happy to receive your letter. Thanks for writing back to me.

It wouldn't hurt to write to Senator Smith. I have an idea I think is better, but I can't tell you about it tonight because Mama says I have to turn out the lights and go to sleep <u>right now</u>.

I'll write more <u>very soon</u>.

Sincerely,
Emily Brewer

CHAPTER SEVEN

"A round-trip ticket to Washington, D.C., please," Emily told the man at the window on Saturday.

He looked up from under his green visor. "Just one?"

Emily studied the dark circles under his eyes, the hint of coffee stains on his thick, sandy-colored mustache. "Yes, sir."

"For you?"

"Yes, sir."

The man chewed the tip of his mustache before speaking "Alone?"

"Yes, sir."

He made a face. "Do you know Washington is thirty-five miles from Baltimore?"

Emily had never thought about the distance, but that didn't matter because the man wasn't expecting an answer. He went right on talking. "I wouldn't let my daughter travel that far alone. Not to a wicked city like Washington. How old are you, anyway?"

She hesitated, wondering if God would punish her for

saying thirteen. She would be thirteen soon. In less than four months.

"Eleven, maybe?" the man prodded.

"I'm twelve and a half!"

He stared at her, his eyes wide and glistening. Like gray marbles shiny with spit. "You sure?"

"I know how old I am!"

"Does your father know you're gallivanting off to Washington all by yourself?"

"My papa is dead, sir."

"Well—" The man cleared his throat. "What about your mother? Does she know where you are?"

Inside her new fur muff, Emily balled her hands together, wondering how to phrase her answer without actually lying. "Sort of."

"Does she or doesn't she?"

"Wel-l-l—Mama doesn't exactly know." From the corner of her eye she could see a group of boys to her left staring at her. There must have been three or four of them, but she was too uncomfortable to look directly at them. She lowered her voice so they wouldn't overhear. "Saturday is the only day I can go to Washington because I have to go to school."

"You think Washington is the kind of place young girls should vacation when they have a day off from school?" the ticket seller asked with a sly wink to the man standing in line behind her.

Emily could hear snickers from the group of boys, but she pretended not to notice. "I'm not going there to vacation. I was on the *Titanic* when it sank, and I need to tell the Senators about the things that went wrong. Senator

William Alden Smith is holding hearings in Washington about the sinking, and I need to tell him I know there weren't enough lifeboats for everyone on board and—"

"Yes, yes," said the man with a dismissive wave of his hand. "Well, I'm sure that the officers from the ship will tell the Senators everything they need to know. Now you run along home to your mama."

Emily leaned forward. "*Oh no, sir!* I've been reading about the hearings in the newspaper. The officers are trying to protect each other. The steerage section was locked, so the third-class passengers couldn't get to the boat deck. And the captain didn't even hold a lifeboat drill the way he was supposed to."

"Listen to Miss Know-It-All," whispered one of the boys nearby.

The group of them cackled like a bunch of crows, and Emily felt her face grow warm.

"She knows more about the *Titanic* than all the officers in the world," said another boy.

Emily turned to frown at the scruffy-looking gang. There were four ruffians in all. The tallest, a boy wearing brown knickers and a gray cap, seemed a year or two older than Emily, and the youngest couldn't have been much older than four. She felt like giving the bunch of them a piece of her mind, but she didn't have any time or energy to waste.

Instead, she removed the coin purse from her fur muff and held it up to the man at the ticket window. "I have money to pay. See? You've got to sell me a ticket to Washington."

Narrowing his eyes, the man took a deep breath. "Well,

you bring me a note from your mother telling me it's all right, and I'll sell you a ticket to Washington. Next!" he called to the man standing behind her.

"But there isn't time!" Emily wailed.

With a rough gesture the man behind her elbowed Emily aside. "You're not the only person in a hurry." He looked at the man at the ticket window. "One for New York."

"Please, sir! You don't understand!" Emily said to the man in the green eyeshade. *"Please!"* She held up the coin purse again, but he ignored her. What could she do now? Emily wondered. Even if she could make Mama understand how important it was for her to go to Washington, Emily couldn't run to Brewer House and back to the station before the train left for Washington.

As she stood considering her next move, the tallest of the four hooligans ambled toward her, leaning so close that she couldn't duck the sour odor of his breath. "You heard him. Go home to your mama."

"Yes," said the tiny boy, who had followed him. "Go home to your mama."

She felt like screaming. She felt like hitting someone. It took all the self-control she could muster to race outside the station and stand on the sidewalk, shaking with frustration under a leaden sky as ugly as her mood.

Someone tapped her gently on the shoulder. "Excuse me, miss," said a young woman. "Could you please tell me the way to Locust Point? The heavens are so soupy this morning, not a speck of the good Lord's blessed sunshine pokes through, and I've lost me sense of direction."

"Um—" said Emily, collecting her wits to respond to the pretty young woman. The girl had rosebud lips and eyes as blue as forget-me-nots. She wore an old-fashioned bonnet, which failed to hide a mass of chestnut-colored hair, and a threadbare coat that came to the tops of her heavy shoes. "I'm not sure exactly," Emily told her. "I used to live in Baltimore when I was little, but I've been overseas nearly four years. I just got back last week."

"Then you landed at Locust Point surely. That's where all the big ocean liners come and go."

"No, we landed in New York, not Baltimore. We were on—"

"Oh," the young woman interrupted. "What's your name?" she inquired unexpectedly.

"Uh—Emily Brewer. I—"

"Maggie Flanagan here. Me and me papa landed at Locust Point ten months ago, but now Papa is—" Her voice broke, and she took a deep breath before continuing. "He's dead and gone, and that's changed everything."

Emily bit her lip, thinking of her own papa's death in Colombo, Ceylon, while her parents were serving as missionaries there. She knew, too, how the death of a parent could change a person's whole life. It was Papa's death that had sent her family home to America, first around the Cape of Good Hope on a tramp steamer and then across the Atlantic—or nearly across the Atlantic—on the *Titanic*.

Maggie was saying something about feeling homesick and defeated, but Emily wasn't really listening. From the corner of her eye she glimpsed the four cheeky boys she had encountered earlier inside the station sauntering outside through the door. The biggest one waved casually to Emily, as if they were friends, and then signaled for the other boys to huddle around him.

Emily chose to ignore the lot of them. "I'm sorry about your papa," she said to Maggie. "Had he been sick long?"

"No. An accident at work. Building railroad cars, he was. He made pretty good money. More than me, anyhow. He was careful to save all he could so as to bring Mama and the little ones to America, but the funeral took most of it. I've no more reason to stay in this unkind city." She held up the worn satchel she was carrying. "I've got everything that's left of me papa's savings in this satchel here, and I'm taking it on the next ship to God's country. County Cork, Ireland."

"Now!" yelled one of the boys, and the four of them swooped upon Maggie and Emily like a plague of locusts. Both girls fell to the ground as the boys disappeared with Emily's fare for Washington, D.C., in her new fur muff and all the savings of Maggie Flanagan's papa in her worn satchel.

Maggie sprang to her feet and chased after the hoodlums. *"Come back! Come back, you wicked devils!"* But Emily, who had been winded in the attack, lay on the pavement unable to move.

By the time Emily recovered her breath and joined the pursuit, Maggie had captured the smallest boy and was shaking him like a dust mop. "What's the name of the boy with my satchel?"

"Ow! You're hurting me."

Maggie shook him again. "What's his name?"

"Let go!"

"I'll let go when you tell me his name."

"Billy."

"Billy what?"

"I don't know! I don't know!"

"You're lying."

"He never told me no last name. Stop squeezing my arm!"

Emily felt something on her cheek. Rain was falling from the pewter-colored sky.

Oblivious to the weather, Maggie hunkered over the boy, so close, their noses almost touched. "Where does he live?" she demanded.

"I don't know. He just offered me a penny if I'd help him steal some purses. I don't know nothing else about him. And now I won't get my penny 'cause I won't be able to find him neither." He started to cry.

"Oh, be gone with you then!" Maggie gave the boy a shove, then stared woodenly as he raced off. "It's raining," she muttered at last. "And I have no money and no place to go."

Chasing after the gang of tough boys, Maggie had seemed much older and stronger than Emily, but now she looked wilted.

It suddenly occurred to Emily that Mama and Cousin Lucretia had their first client. "Yes, you do. I'm taking you to Brewer House. Hurry now before we get sopped."

CHAPTER EIGHT

Although the rooms inside were so large that Mama referred to Brewer House as a mansion, Emily considered the outside as ordinary as the row house half a mile away that she and her family were renting next to Mrs. Lieberman's. Four marble steps to an unimposing redbrick building.

By the time she and Maggie Flanagan reached their destination, the sun had forced its way through bleak clouds. Steam rose from the flat roof of Brewer House. The exterior bricks of the old mansion no longer seemed sooty and mournful, as they had on Emily's previous visits to the site, but now looked almost rosy.

Emily opened the front door and entered first, motioning for Maggie to follow behind.

Pee-yoo! thought Emily. The interior smelled of turpentine and lye soap.

"Mama!" she called. "Where are you?"

"In here. The dining room."

Emily *clip-clop*ped ahead of Maggie a few paces down

the hardwood floor of the hall and turned right through the archway into the dining room. There, above dark wainscoting, freshly hung wallpaper—in a dizzying pattern of green pampas grass against an orange background—circled most of the room. Buckets, tatters of paper, and dirty rags littered the floor.

Bent over a makeshift table of loose boards set on wooden sawhorses, Mama and Cousin Lucretia were slathering paste on the back of a length of wallpaper. Mama looked up. "You're supposed to be home looking after your brother and sister," she said accusingly. "What are you doing here?"

Emily had anticipated that question and had silently practiced her answer. "Mrs. Lieberman told me that Sarah and Robert hadn't given her any trouble all week and I should spend my Saturday at the library trying to get caught up with the other pupils at school." It hadn't occurred to Mrs. Lieberman, nor had Emily bothered to tell her, that she was far less interested in catching up with the unexceptional students in her seventh-grade class than in going to Washington, D.C., and telling Senator William Alden Smith a few things he needed to know about the *Titanic*.

"Oh, hello," Mama said to Maggie when she realized Emily wasn't alone. She stood up straight, trying to poke a loose strand of hair back into the ash-blond topknot resting like a scrawny sparrow upon her head. The gesture left a daub of paste on Mama's forehead, which Emily decided not to mention.

Mama wiped both hands on the sides of her long apron before holding the right one out toward the new girl.

"I'm Emily's mother. And this is my husband's cousin, Lucretia Brewer."

Cousin Lucretia stood up too. She was taller than Mama, and at least fifty pounds heavier. Her watery blue eyes were set in a moon-shaped face. "How do you do?" she said.

Maggie took Mama's proffered hand. "Pleased to meet you both, I'm sure. I'm Maggie Flanagan."

"Why, you're soaking wet," said Mama. "And you are too, Emily. Take your coats into the kitchen and hang them over the backs of the chairs near the stove. And put another lump of coal in the fire while you're at it."

"But we need to talk to you," Emily protested.

Maggie nodded in agreement. "Emily here rescued me. Or tried to. The honest truth, though, is that I'm still in a bit of trouble. A gang of hooligans stole Emily's beautiful fur muff and me own satchel containing every stitch and farthing I own."

"Everything?" asked Cousin Lucretia. Her puffy cheeks seemed redder than usual. The first time Emily had met her, she had noticed that Cousin Lucretia's eyes disappeared into those puffy cheeks when she smiled, but she wasn't smiling now.

Emily nodded. "I promised Maggie you two would help her. She doesn't have any money or a job or anywhere to sleep tonight. She needs—"

"You can tell us about it as soon as you've warmed up a bit. You'll catch your deaths standing around in those drippy coats." Mama pointed toward the kitchen. "Go in by the stove."

"We'll sit down there with you as soon as we hang this one strip of wallpaper," said Cousin Lucretia. "We have to get it on the wall before the paste dries."

"When was the last time you ate?" Mama asked Maggie.

"I had some toast yesterday."

"Goodness!" said Cousin Lucretia. "You must be starving."

"Emily," instructed Mama, "give her some of those raisin muffins I brought over here this morning. They're in the bread box on the countertop."

"I'm sure you could do with a cup of tea too," added Cousin Lucretia. "We all could. Emily, after you give the coals a good stoking, heat a pot of water for some tea."

In the kitchen, Emily stoked the fire, hung up their coats on the backs of two chairs, and filled the blue-speckled teakettle with water while Maggie wolfed down two raisin muffins. Soon the four of them were sitting around the wobbly white table, listening to Maggie's story about her life in County Cork, Ireland, as the oldest of four children.

She described how her papa's work in a foundry was unsteady, and the family, even the youngest children, often went to bed hungry. Dreaming of taking their family to America, the land of plenty, her parents tried to borrow money from her papa's uncle, but he lent them only enough for two steerage passages. So it was agreed that Maggie and her papa would come first and work hard to repay the debt, and then bring the rest of the family over.

"Her papa had just saved enough when he was killed building railroad cars," explained Emily.

"Papa always said America was the land of promise, but

it's been broken promises, if you ask me," Maggie continued. "I expected to find a job where I could hold up me head and be treated like a decent lady, selling in a department store maybe, but the snooty store managers all said I was too young."

"How old are you?" Mama asked.

"I'm fourteen now, but was just thirteen when me and Papa arrived last June."

"You're only two years older than I am!" said Emily. "I thought you were at least eighteen or nineteen."

"I've aged a lot in the ten months I've been here. Had to in service to that pinched-faced Mrs. Huffaker."

"In service?" asked Emily.

"A maid, I guess you'd call me. More like a slave, though. She hardly paid me enough to buy stamps for letters home to me mum. It was nothing to the missus, it wasn't, to wake me after dark, when I'd finally got into a sound sleep, to rescrub a floor she didn't think I'd done right."

"Hmmph," said Cousin Lucretia.

"Seven days a week I worked, with only two hours off on Sunday afternoons. But at least I had a warm bed and two meals a day. So I didn't mind as long as Papa was alive. We met every Sunday afternoon, in the park when the weather was warm enough, or a little café across the street when it wasn't." Maggie sighed. "Those were the good times I looked forward to."

"You said he made pretty good money," Emily reminded Maggie.

Maggie nodded. "Thirteen dollars a week. He kept five

dollars for his own room and board—things are expensive here in Baltimore—and sent home six to repay his uncle and for Mum and the little ones to live on. Most weeks he saved the rest. I found it under his mattress, where he'd told me he kept it, after his accident. But I had to spend nearly half of it to bury him proper. I was on me way to Locust Point to book passage on the next ship to Ireland so I could take what money was left home to Mum. But then those hooligans—" She swallowed. "Now all of Papa's savings is gone."

Cousin Lucretia drummed her fingers on the pockmarked tabletop. "I could lend you enough to buy a steerage passage home to Ireland. If that's what you want to do."

"I—I don't know," said Maggie. "Work is tight back home. Anything I earned, if I could find me a job, would have to go to feeding Mum and the little ones. I don't suppose I could ever repay you."

"Well, I don't suppose that's too impor—" Cousin Lucretia began.

"Why don't you stay here?" Emily suggested. "You said your family wanted to come to America. You could stay here and work until you've saved enough money to bring everyone here."

Mama put some sugar in her tea and stirred it with a spoon. "That may be easier said than done. It took her father ten months to save enough money. And women in America don't earn a fraction of what men do."

"No, but things is even worse in Ireland," said Maggie. "Maybe you're right. Maybe I should stay here. If I go home, Mum will just have another empty stomach to fret about."

"Until something better turns up, you can always go back to Mrs. Huffaker," said Mama. "At least you have food and a warm bed there."

"No." Maggie paused. "I can't go back there."

Something about her tone of voice alarmed the others. Mama stopped stirring her tea and held her spoon in midair. Cousin Lucretia stared at the girl from above the rims of her glasses. Emily hunched forward, waiting for Maggie to go on.

"She—she let me go."

"Fired you?" asked Emily.

Maggie nodded.

"How come?" demanded Emily.

"It was all a terrible misunderstanding. This morning the mister—her husband—wanted me to shine his shoes, but I was in me bedroom worrying about me problems. Crying, you might say." Maggie bit her lip, again on the verge of tears.

Mama waited a moment, until Maggie seemed calmer. "What happened?"

"He knocked on me door, and when he saw how upset I was, he wanted to know what was wrong. So I told him that tomorrow would be me first Sunday without Papa, and I didn't know how I could stand living in America all alone, without even me Sunday afternoons with Papa to look forward to. He put an arm around me—just to comfort me, nothing else—it wasn't much more than you're doing this minute—but right then the missus walked by. She screamed at me—accused me of being a home wrecker and called me all kinds of wicked names that I wouldn't dare repeat in polite society. Oh, it was awful!" With that, Maggie broke into full sobs.

With a smile of encouragement, Mama pulled a handkerchief from the pocket of her apron and handed it to Maggie. "Take your time. We can wait." Emily opened her mouth to say something, but Mama shot her a dark look.

After a moment, Maggie wiped her eyes for one last time and squeezed the soiled handkerchief into a ball on her lap. "I have to admit that I've had enough of being in service, if working for Mrs. Huffaker is any example of what that means in America. The only way I'd want to stay in Baltimore is to find another kind of work."

Cousin Lucretia was scraping some dried wallpaper paste from a fingernail. "Well, you are a bit young to sell in a department store."

"Is there anything else you can do?" said Mama. "Is there anything your mother taught you?"

"I can sew a bit."

Mama smiled. "You've come to the right place for that. Baltimore is the men's garment capital of America."

"Yes, but no one in the factories here speaks English. I tried lots of places when I first came to the city—Papa even went with me to help—but no one understood us when we asked to speak to the managers."

"That could be a problem, all right," said Cousin Lucretia. "All the garment factories here are owned by German Jews who speak Yiddish."

"And they hire only Yiddish-speakers?" asked Mama.

Cousin Lucretia nodded. "I think so."

"That doesn't seem right," argued Emily. "You don't have to speak Yiddish to know how to sew."

Cousin Lucretia spread her fingers to study the condition of all her nails before going to work on another one. "No, but immigrants tend to stick together and help each other out. Many of the first German Jews who arrived in Baltimore were tailors and seamstresses. As soon as they were able to save enough money, they bought their own factories and hired workers who had just arrived from Germany. New immigrants aren't in a hurry to learn English, because there's no need to." She turned to Maggie. "Did you try Herman Bamberger's factory?"

Maggie shrugged. "I couldn't rightly say. Might have. At the time, it seemed like a million places I went."

"Bamberger's has the best reputation," said Cousin Lucretia. "I understand that it's the cleanest of the shops. And Herman Bamberger doesn't believe in child labor. He never hires anyone under fourteen, although all the other factories in this city regularly break the law, I'm told. Bamberger even allows the men who work for him to belong to a union."

Mama nodded. "That's pretty forward-looking."

"Yes, but I don't suppose the women are treated as well. They never are," said Cousin Lucretia. "Anyway, I don't have any influence with Bamberger. Wish I did. The only person I know in the garment business is Otto Meyer. I can't say I'd recommend working for him, though. That old skinflint would sell his grandmother's dentures if someone offered him a nickel."

"Why do you say that?" Mama asked.

Cousin Lucretia rubbed her hands together to get rid of any lingering dust from the wallpaper paste. "When Father was still alive, he lent Otto money from an inheritance to open his first factory. Never asked him for interest or made him sign any papers. They just shook hands. A gentlemen's agreement, Father called it. Otto was slow with the payments each month, and he'd paid off less than half before Father died, even though he bought his wife a new house and took his whole family to Europe in first-class accommodations. Mother assumed Otto would pay off the remainder of the debt to her, but he never did."

"Didn't she ask him about it?" Mama wanted to know.

"Yes, but he said the agreement had been with Father, not her, and she had no right to expect it. That's what he considered a gentlemen's agreement, I guess."

"That was a long time ago," said Mama. "Maybe Mr. Meyer has changed."

"As a matter of fact, I had an encounter with him after your husband died, and I decided to raise money for Brewer House." Cousin Lucretia brushed the paste dust from her lap to the floor. "I had seen him driving a new Packard exactly like mine, so I knew what he had paid for it. I also knew that he was building another home, an even larger one, so I decided it was time he repaid the debt he owed my father. I called on him very courteously, buttering him up by remarking about what a splendid citizen he is, and I asked him for a fifty-dollar donation. You would have thought I had asked him for fifty thousand. He carried on so about how hard it was for him to meet his payroll and to cover the cost of electricity to run the machines in his sweatshop, that I was afraid the old tightwad might drown in his crocodile tears."

"Sweatshop?" said Maggie.

"Sweatshop is the expression for any factory that exploits its workers. The worst ones are small businesses that contract for piecework," Mama explained.

"Yes," Cousin Lucretia agreed. "I think Meyer's sweatshop just helps larger factories fill their orders when they're under special deadlines."

Emily felt the conversation needed to get back to Maggie's problems. "Hiring someone isn't the same as making a donation," she argued. "Couldn't you ask Mr. Meyer to give Maggie a chance?"

"I certainly don't mind asking him, but I can't guarantee that he would hire her. Or that Maggie would enjoy working for him even if he did. Those places are called sweatshops for good reason. The workers put in long hours for very little money."

"But they don't have to work at night, and part of Sunday too, do they, the way Maggie did for Mrs. Huffaker?" Emily said. She turned to Maggie. "You'd like sewing in a sweatshop better than being in service, wouldn't you?"

Maggie nodded. "Yes."

"Wonderful," said Emily. "I'm sure Cousin Lucretia can help you. That's why she's building this place, to help people like you. You can stay in Baltimore and save money to bring your family over. And until you have a place of your own, you can stay with us. You can share my bed with me."

"You know she can't do that," Mama said. "Our home is under quarantine until Sarah gets over her scarlet fever. Anyone who hasn't already had the disease can't visit even for a few minutes."

"Have you had scarlet fever?" Emily asked Maggie.

"Yes. Two years ago."

"Then it's all settled!" Emily exclaimed. "I mean it is, isn't it, Mama?"

Mama let out a sigh. "Yes, yes. I suppose."

CHAPTER NINE

McLean, Virginia
May 4, 1912

Dear Emily,

    I didn't write to Senator Smith about the "Titanic" because you said you had a better idea and would write me about it "<u>very soon</u>."
    I've been waiting and waiting to hear what your idea is. Now I'm worried sick. Are you all right? You didn't catch scarlet fever, did you? Didn't you tell me you had already had it? Did something worse happen to you?
    Please write back!

                    Your friend,
                    Albert

P.S. If you can't write, maybe your mother will let me know what has happened to you.

CHAPTER TEN

Baltimore, Maryland
May 10, 1912

Dear Albert,

No, I'm not sick or anything. I'm sorry you were worried about me. I didn't write sooner because I've been <u>terribly</u> busy. Besides doing my lessons and watching after Robert and Sarah (she is still recovering from her scarlet fever), I've spent lots of time with my new friends. I never thought I'd have any friends in Baltimore, but I have two! (Imagine!) Having friends to talk to makes me feel better in the daytime and also at night. I still have bad dreams, but not as often.

My friend at school is Louise Kezerian. The other girls don't like her, but I do. They say she's fat and a tomboy, and they don't like the way she talks, which is sometimes sarcastic, like a boy. (Remember how you talked to me when we first met?) I don't really mind when she says mean things, because I know she's lonely and just wants attention. Besides, she doesn't really talk that way to me anymore because we're friends now.

Louise and I eat lunch together every day and walk partway home from school. (She lives in a big house about a mile from the row house where our family lives.)

Right now Louise is planning a really exciting party for her birthday on June 8, so everyone is being nice to her. She knows they're being two-faced, but she'll probably invite most of them to her party anyway. It's going to be the fanciest party that anyone in our school has ever been to, but she hasn't told anyone else exactly what it will be. (I'm the only one who knows, but I can't tell you yet because I promised.)

My other friend is named Maggie Flanagan, and she's actually living with me! We share a bedroom. Really! It hasn't been two weeks since I met her, just after her papa died, but I feel as if I've known her my whole life. She's fourteen, two years older than I am. Sometimes she seems much older than that, and sometimes she seems much younger. One of the things she seems younger about is her grammar. It's even worse than Robert's. Papa would be horrified to hear a fourteen-year-old make the mistakes Maggie does. He always said you can tell a lady by her grammar. (I used to believe that too, but I don't anymore.)

I love to hear Maggie talk because she has an Irish brogue. It's a good thing I like to listen, because she likes to talk. She talks and talks and talks. She also has a wonderful singing voice. Whenever we wash the dishes together, we teach each other silly songs. If Sarah and Robert aren't around, we tell each other secrets.

The reason Maggie seems older is that she works. She has to support herself because her papa died and the rest of her family still lives in County Cork. She makes buttonholes in a men's garment sweatshop (that's what people call a small factory that doesn't treat its workers well). I guess the reason she talks so much to me is that, except for the owner, who never mingles with the workers, she has met only one other person in the factory who speaks English. That is a little nine-year-old girl named Ruth Weinstein. She and Maggie sit together whenever they can. Ruth is too young to sew handmade buttonholes the way Maggie does. She can't operate any of the machines either. She just cuts loose threads with scissors and runs errands for the older workers. Can you believe that she works all day, six days a week, and earns barely enough to pay for her own food?

Ruth's father works upstairs in the same factory, but he doesn't speak English. He's a cutter, which is the highest-paid worker in the sweatshop, but he doesn't earn enough to support a family of six. It's against the law for nine-year-olds to work, but Ruth does anyway. (I think she should go to school, don't you?) When the labor inspector comes to the factory, Ruth hides in a box under lots of heavy fabric. It's hard for her to breathe there, but she has to stay until the inspector leaves.

Can you imagine a family being so poor that they have to send their children to work at age nine? I thought something like that could happen only in countries like Ceylon and India. But I'm learning that there's lots of poverty in Ireland, where Maggie comes from, and Baltimore too!

I almost forgot the main reason I'm writing this letter. You wanted to know what my wonderful idea was about the "Titanic." I'm afraid it didn't turn out to be too wonderful. I had planned to go to the Capitol in Washington, D.C., to speak to Senator William Alden Smith in person. He needs to hear _from_ _someone who was on the ship but doesn't have to protect the_ _White Star Line_ about all the things that went wrong on the "Titanic." (Our landlady offered to watch Sarah and Robert so I could leave the house.) I got as far as Camden Station (that's where I met Maggie), but the ticket seller wouldn't let me have a ticket. He acted as if I were a child or something, just because I'm a girl. I was mad enough to chew railroad spikes!

I'm sure a ticket seller wouldn't treat you the way that man treated me. You're a year older and <u>you're a male</u>! Anyhow, you live lots closer to Washington than I do. Does your grandmother have a motorcar? Maybe she can drive you there. I hope you'll go right away—before the hearings are over. (That could be any day now.)

Tell Senator Smith and his committee all the things that went wrong on the ship and that I will back up everything you say. (You can give him my address and tell him to contact me if he wants.) Then write back and tell me everything that happens at the hearing.

Sincerely,
Emily

P.S. I'll be able to tell you the plans for Louise Kezerian's birthday party soon.

P.P.S. I hope I'm not boring you with this long, long letter. I'm writing you such a long one because I don't have anything better to do tonight. Maggie isn't home from work yet. Sometimes she works as late as nine o'clock or even nine-thirty. If she were home, she'd probably be teaching me a new song, or I'd be helping her with reading or grammar lessons. She needs me to help her because she went to school less than two years in Ireland.

CHAPTER ELEVEN

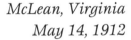

> McLean, Virginia
> May 14, 1912

Emily,

I'm happy to know that you have so many wonderful new friends, and I'm sure you'll have a magnificent time at Louise's party, which promises to be the most exciting social event in the history of Baltimore, Maryland, or possibly the entire United States of America. From now on, I'm sure you'll be much too busy to write further letters to tone-deaf (and sarcastic) males who worry just because you don't answer their letters promptly, so this will be the last letter I send you.

I'm just as busy as you are, maybe even busier. I can't travel to Washington, D.C., to talk to Senator William Alden Smith just because you think I should.

Here are a few of the reasons why I'm too busy to go to Washington:

1. *After the "Titanic" sank with Mother aboard, my little sister Virginia became an orphan, so I'm the only real family she has left. Ginny's father died nine months ago, before we moved to London, and now she doesn't have a mother <u>or</u> father. (I'm an orphan now too, in case you hadn't noticed.)*
2. *When I told Ginny about Mother's death after the "Carpathia" rescued us, I promised her that I would never leave her as long as she needed me.*
3. *Ginny is too sick to be abandoned now, even if I hadn't made that promise. I remind you that she has scarlet fever (which she caught from your little sister).*
4. *Grandmother has been crying so much about Uncle Claybourne that she doesn't spend much time with Ginny.*
5. *Mattie Lou, our housekeeper, is too busy with her cooking and cleaning to take care of Ginny.*
6. *Abraham, our manservant, is busy in the yard, so he doesn't have time to run errands for Ginny.*
7. *I'm busy starting my own project about the "Titanic."*

In case you're interested (probably not), I'll tell you about number 7 above. I found the names and Washington addresses of all the U.S. Senators, and I'm going to start writing to them just as soon as I finish this letter. Which is right now.

Good-bye,
Albert Mason Trask, Jr.

CHAPTER TWELVE

"This mush tastes funny," six-year-old Sarah announced.

"Mmm," Emily replied absently, staring at the paper she was holding.

"I said this mush tastes funny," Sarah repeated louder.

Emily looked up, suddenly noticing her little sister. "You're still in your nightgown, and your hair isn't combed. Do you realize how disgusting it is to come to the breakfast table looking that way?"

"Robert's hair isn't combed either. And he still has on his nightshirt. You're too busy reading that letter from your boyfriend to help him dress. Anyway, I'm sick. Mama says sick people need their rest. They wear their nightclothes all the time because they have to stay in bed."

"Are not sick," said Robert, swinging his little bare feet back and forth. Since the family's arrival in Baltimore, two-and-a-half-year-old Robert had miraculously recovered from the ailment that had sapped his energy in Ceylon and left him wilted on their travels across two oceans. He'd also discovered that he enjoyed arguing. "The sick sign isn't in the window anymore. So there!"

It was true. A nurse from the health department had examined Sarah at the house yesterday and told Mama she could remove the quarantine sign from the front window.

"Well?" persisted Sarah. "Aren't you going to do anything?"

"About what?" said Emily, distracted by worry over Albert's letter. She had read it three times after the postman had brought it yesterday and twice again this morning. Was Albert really as angry as the letter sounded? Why? What had she said in her letter to him that he could possibly have misinterpreted?

"The mush. It tastes burned," said Sarah.

"That's because you and Robert didn't come when I called you to breakfast two hours ago," Emily explained. "The oatmeal got stuck to the bottom of the pan when I tried to heat it again. Put some more sugar on it and you won't notice the taste."

Robert pounded the contents of his bowl with the back of his spoon. "It has bumps. I don't like bumps."

"Eat it anyway," Emily said. "A few lumps won't hurt you."

"No." Robert pounded the cereal harder. "I don't eat bumps. Mama don't make me eat bumps."

"You mean Mama *doesn't* make you eat bumps," Emily said.

Grinning, Robert waved his spoon in the air. "See? I told you!"

Emily wasn't amused. "Mama isn't here now. She's gone

to Brewer House to help Cousin Lucretia hang more wall-paper. And Maggie has gone to work. I'm in charge now, and I say eat your cereal."

"No."

"Then drink your milk."

"No."

"All right," said Emily. "Then go hungry."

"No. I want mush with no bumps." He resumed pound-ing. "No bumps. No bumps. No bumps."

Emily frowned, not so much at her grumpy little brother and sister as at Albert's letter. What did he mean about not writing to each other anymore? Did he think she didn't want to? She refolded the letter and put it back into the pocket of the smock Mrs. Lieberman had given her. The landlady had said that Emily was going to ruin the dresses Cousin Lucretia had given her by wearing them after school and on Saturdays. So Mrs. Lieberman had provided Emily with some loose-fitting old cotton smocks to wear over them.

Sarah swallowed a mouthful of resugared cereal and pointed with her spoon. "What's that?"

"Hmm?" said Emily.

"That pail," said Sarah. "Did Maggie forget her lunch?"

Emily looked in the direction Sarah was pointing. There, resting on the shoddy linoleum near the icebox, was Maggie's round black lunch pail. "Oh dear!" said Emily, so engrossed for the moment in Maggie's problem that she put aside her own worries about Albert's letter.

Maggie had been so late getting up this morning that she had taken time only for a few swallows of tea before leaving for work at six a.m. If she didn't have anything to eat at noon, she would go twenty-four hours without any food. Although Maggie never complained about her job (at least not in front of Mama or Mrs. Lieberman), Emily knew that it was grueling work. Maggie always arrived home with a backache and sore fingers. She needed some bread and fruit at noon to sustain her through the ten, twelve, even fourteen hours she had to work each day.

Emily scowled at her brother and sister, who refused to eat a perfectly good breakfast. Lots of people in this world were hungry—beggars in Ceylon, homeless people in Baltimore, even workers in sweatshops, like Ruth Weinstein and Maggie Flanagan. She'd bet they would be grateful for a bowl of oatmeal right now.

"You're frowning," Robert told her, and he began singing a song that Maggie had taught him:

Be a style, be a style,
Be a style, be a style.

"You're not singing the right words," complained Sarah. She sang it for him:

Frowning, frowning all the while—
Everyone prefers a smile.
Change that frown into a smile,
Smile, smile, be in style,
Be in style, be in style.

"That wasn't what you sang."

"Was too," said Robert. "That's what Maggie said: *Be a style, be a style,*" he sang.

"Was not," said Sarah. "It doesn't make sense to 'be a style,' does it, Emily?"

Emily didn't respond, so Sarah answered her own question. "You never get the words to songs right. You're supposed to say, 'Change that frown into a smile/Smile, smile, be in style.'"

"Be a style," sang Robert. *"Be a style, be a style, be a style—"*

Ignoring both the boy soprano and his self-appointed music critic, Emily considered what she should do about Maggie's lunch pail. She had seen the bedraggled black-and-white sign some two miles away, signaling the location of Otto Meyer's garment factory, and knew where Maggie went each day. But what good did that information do her?

Emily couldn't exactly leave Sarah and Robert home alone while she walked to the sweatshop and back. The trip could take forty-five minutes each way, not counting any time she might spend at the factory. She didn't have money to take the trolley. And she certainly couldn't expect Mrs. Lieberman to take care of the children today. The landlady, who watched the children every day while Emily was in school, was not home. Besides, now that Sarah was over her scarlet fever and Robert no longer had the strange ailment he had caught in Ceylon, Mrs. Lieberman had complained yesterday that the children were getting "too full of spizzerinktum for an old lady to watch."

The only alternative was for Emily to take Sarah and Robert with her to the sweatshop. She groaned inwardly,

thinking about dragging Robert along by a hand or carrying him much of the way, but there was no other choice.

"Wash your face and get dressed," she told Sarah. "I'll
brush and comb your hair. Robert, go find the sailor suit
Cousin Lucretia bought you, and I'll help you put it on."

"Do I have to?" whined Sarah. "I don't know why I
always have to comb my hair when no one ever sees me."

"Today you're going to see lots of people. You're all
better. The nurse said it was all right for you to leave the
house now."

Sarah's face brightened. "You mean I can go outside?"

Emily nodded. "Mmm-hmm. And it's such a beautiful
day, I think we should go on a nice long May walk.
Wouldn't that be fun?"

"Oh, yes! We can take Maggie's lunch pail with us and
visit her in the factory," said Sarah, as if that were her
own idea.

"We can sing to her," suggested Robert. He picked up
the lunch pail by its handle, clanging it with his spoon as he
stomped around the linoleum in his tiny bare feet. *"Be a
style, be a style, be a style—"*

CHAPTER THIRTEEN

Sarah pinched her nostrils shut with a thumb and fore-finger. "Eee-yoo. Let's hurry and find Maggie so we can go home."

Robert was more direct. "It's stinky here."

None of the workers could possibly hear her brother's little voice above all the whirring, thrumming, droning, trilling, and wailing noises of the various machines in this room as they churned out parts of new jackets and vests for men. And the workers certainly didn't need Robert to tell them about the vile stench of the place. It seemed to be a combination of some of the foulest odors on the planet—human waste, insecticide, and rotting garbage, not to mention the smell of decaying flesh. Emily had learned to recognize that last odor in Ceylon, where it usually indicated an infestation of mice and rats.

Sarah studied the floor, littered with bits of fabric, paper, cardboard, and unidentifiable clutter. She squeezed her sister's arm. "Let's hurry and go home."

"In a minute," said Emily, searching around the workplace for Maggie's familiar mop of curly chestnut-colored hair.

In a room not too much bigger than her classroom at school, at least forty workers (all women, it seemed) were seated shoulder to shoulder on either side of five long tables. Dirty windows on one side of the room admitted barely enough light for the seamstresses seated next to them to do their work, let alone the workers farther away. Some of the women were sewing by hand, and some were operating machines, but all the faces Emily could see wore expressions of drudgery and despair.

Like Sarah, Emily was tempted to turn around and leave this horrible place, but she had dragged her little brother and sister all the way here, and she was determined to find Maggie. Biting her lip, she took a few steps into the room. Sarah followed cautiously behind, but Robert strode up to the first woman by the door and tugged at her skirt.

"Hey!" He pointed overhead. "You didn't turn the lights on."

Emily looked up. Along the length of the high ceiling were six long metal tubes, which she assumed to be casings for electric wires that powered the machines. Perpendicular to those tubes were two shorter ones from which were suspended four unlit electric lightbulbs. Cousin Lucretia had told her that Otto Meyer was cheap, but Emily couldn't believe he didn't know the women would do better work if they could see what they were doing.

The woman Robert had approached blinked, as if not

accustomed to being interrupted at her work. She paused a moment before speaking. *"Ich farshtai nit."*

Dissatisfied with that response, Robert tried a question. "Where's Maggie?"

She cupped a hand to her ear and leaned forward. *"Ret pavoli."*

Emily stepped to Robert's side and rested her hand on his shoulder. From farther away the woman's haggard face had made her seem almost as old as Emily's teacher, Miss Cameron. But now that Emily had walked closer, she could see that the seamstress wasn't much older than Maggie, possibly seventeen or eighteen. Over her dress she wore a loose-fitting smock cut from a pattern similar to the one that Emily was wearing. Made of checked gingham, it had a scoop neckline, narrow yoke, and gathered skirt.

Robert repeated his question, louder than before. "Where's Maggie?"

The woman, or girl, if that's what she was, looked toward Emily for help. *"Ich farshtai nit."*

"She doesn't speak English," Emily whispered to her brother. "Look for a little girl." She held out her hand to indicate someone just a little taller than Sarah. "She's a friend of Maggie's named Ruth. She can probably help us."

Full of the "spizzerinktum" that had worn Mrs. Lieberman out, Robert started to dart off, but just then Sarah spotted their friend. She grabbed Robert's arm. "There's Maggie!"

"Where?"

"Against the wall!"

"Yes, there's Maggie!" Robert echoed. He trotted off in

Maggie's direction, tripped over something on the floor, and scrambled to his feet again as Emily and Sarah followed. "Maggie! Maggie! Maggie!"

"Robert! What are you doing here?" Maggie asked, and then realized he wasn't alone. She smiled at Emily. "Oh, it's me lunch. May the saints bless you. I didn't know how I was to get through this long day without a bite of food. I'm hungry already."

"I told you *Tateh* would give you a piece of our bread," said a small girl sitting on a stool next to her. With a pair of scissors she was clipping loose threads from a man's suit jacket. "You always give extras to me."

"Such as they are, such as they are," said Maggie. "I eat like a pack of wolves at noontime, I do," she explained to Emily. "Ruth, I'd like you to meet me friends here. These are the folks who took me in when I didn't have a place to lay me poor head. Emily. Sarah. Robert." Ruth exchanged nods with them, one by one.

"Can we go now?" Sarah asked her sister.

"Yes, you better go," said Maggie, suddenly agitated as a man dressed in a three-piece suit strode toward them. His full black beard failed to hide the surly expression on his face.

"Is that Mr. Meyer?" asked Emily. "He looks younger than I thought he would."

"No, that's the foreman, Mr. Epstein, and the one's just as sour as the other," Maggie whispered. "Two halves of the same persimmon, if you ask me. The only difference is that Mr. Epstein can't speak English and Mr. Meyer won't, at least not for lollygagging with the likes of me. But I know what the pair of them is thinking, just by the way they snarl."

Sarah shifted her weight from one foot to the other. "I want to go home."

"Yes." Maggie swept her head to indicate all three Brewers. "You'd best be on your way. Hurry now, before that bucket of gloom sees you talking to me and Ruth."

But the man striding toward them had already seen the visitors. His eyes flashed with anger as he shouted at Ruth and pointed to a box across the room, then disappeared up the stairway.

"What did he want?" Maggie asked her.

"He said for me to get rid of my visitors and take more fabric to the cutters."

"Tell him it's me these folks have come to see," said Maggie. "Tell him it's me whose lunch pail was plumb forgot this morning."

Ruth shook her head. "Don't worry. But I better do what he says. And you better go," she told Emily. Dashing off, she ran to the box the foreman had indicated, hefted a huge bundle of cloth—too big for a child that size, Emily felt—and struggled toward the stairs.

"I'm sorry if we got you into trouble," Emily told Maggie.

Maggie waved a hand in front of her face. "Tsh. I'm glad you had the chance to meet Ruth. Isn't she a love? I've been blathering at her for the whole of two weeks, telling her what a joy your family has been to me, even those two busy little troublemakers you're minding. . . . Oh look, would you! Robert's trying to chase up those stairs after Ruth!"

"Robert!" called Emily. "Come back!"

"Robert, come back!" Sarah echoed. "We need to go home!" she added.

The boy was now out of sight, so Emily started after him. But no sooner had she taken a few steps than a blood-curdling shriek rang out from above. *"Tateh! Tateh! Oy, gevalt!"*

"Ruth!" cried a man upstairs, followed by a babble of excited male voices.

"Something's wrong!" cried Maggie. She sprang to her feet and shoved Emily against the wall to race up the stairs ahead of her two at a time.

Sarah rushed to join Emily at the base of the stairs, but by the time the two of them reached the cutting room in the second story, all production there had stopped. Five male workers had left their pressing and cutting machines to cluster together in a knot of anxious chatter. Three other men were quarreling, their voices rising.

Hunkered over like an old lady, Ruth was shaking with sobs. The front of her dress was turning red as she bunched a fistful of the cloth around her right hand with her left. Blood had spurted over everything on one of the cutting-room tables. The blade, the arm of the machine, the thick layers of fabric—all were spattered with something almost the color of tomato sauce.

"Oy, gevalt! Oy, gevalt!" wailed Ruth.

Crouched beside her young friend, Maggie was half biting, half tearing her petticoat into strips.

"What are you doing?" Emily cried. "What's going on?"

Maggie didn't look up. "She needs a tourniquet. She cut off her thumb."

For the first time Emily noticed the severed digit lying on the table. She took a deep breath, afraid she might faint.

"Oh, no-o-o," moaned Sarah.

"How did it happen?" said Emily.

Maggie continued to shred her petticoat. "I don't know."

"Rat," said Robert. When no one paid him any attention, he spoke louder. "Naughty rat. Naughty bad rat." Still no one cared, so Robert tried pointing. "See?"

Emily wondered what Robert had seen, if anything. She bent down to him. "Did you see a rat scare Ruth? Did it try to bite her?"

"Bad rat," said Robert. "Naughty, bad rat."

Maggie's voice was raspy as she spoke to Emily. "Help me, will you?"

"What do you want me to do?"

"Hold her arm out while I wrap this tourniquet around. No, no, take her by the wrist."

Ruth shrieked in pain as Emily pulled the girl's right hand from the clump of fabric in her left. "Be brave," Emily whispered.

A softer moan escaped as Ruth squeezed her eyes shut and clenched her teeth.

"There now, I'm done with that part, love," Maggie said at last. "Now I'll put this other bandage around your hand. I won't make it tight like the other one. How's that?"

"It hurts. It hurts," wailed Ruth.

"I know. But you're a very brave girl, love," said Maggie.

"Your papa will get you to a hospital, and the doctor will give you something for the pain. There's a love now."

"I feel sick," said Sarah.

"You're not the one who's hurt," Emily snapped, but when she turned to see the expression on Sarah's face, she wished she had been more understanding. Her little sister had turned green. "Run outside!" Emily ordered. "Quick! Run outside!"

Sarah was already on her way toward the stairs, her hand clamped tightly over her mouth.

Robert was pointing toward a ball of fur huddled against the wall. "See? There it is."

"There what is?" asked Emily.

"Rat. There. It climbed up her leg," Robert explained.

Having spent three years in Ceylon, Emily knew about the habits of rodents and how their sudden movements could startle anyone. Accidents like Ruth's were bound to happen in a place full of dangerous machinery, especially if mice and rats were allowed to roam. A rat might have frightened her so that she had put her hand down on the table beside the cutting blade.

A little child like Ruth shouldn't have to work in a dump like this, Emily thought, but neither should Maggie. Or anyone else for that matter. She wondered where she could go to report Otto Meyer. He should be forced to clean up this filthy place. Maybe some time in jail would teach him a lesson.

"*Zol Got mir helfen!*" implored a male voice.

Emily turned. A shabbily dressed man, one of the three

who had been arguing, dropped to his knees to plead with the foreman and the third man, who was no doubt Mr. Meyer. The man on his knees folded his hands together near his chin as he pleaded with the owner.

"What's going on?" Emily asked Ruth.

"Tateh says the accident . . . wasn't . . . his fault." It was such an effort for Ruth to talk that Emily could barely understand her words. "Mameh . . . and the children . . . will . . . go hungry."

Emily frowned at the men. How could these men waste time arguing when Ruth was desperate to see a doctor?

Maggie charged over to them. "Mr. Meyer, can you have your discussion later? Ruth's father has to get her to a hospital right now."

"Yes, yes," said Mr. Meyer. "Go on, Weinstein." With a sweeping motion of his arm he repeated the instruction to Ruth's father in words Emily couldn't understand.

Mr. Weinstein clutched the owner's trousers. *"Ich bet eich bitteh!"* he begged.

"Let go, Weinstein!" raged Mr. Meyer.

"What's the matter?" Maggie asked. "Why isn't he coming? Doesn't he have money for a taxi?"

"I told him I'd pay for a taxi. But it's a business I'm running here. What does he expect? Someone has to pay for all the material that was ruined. Quality material, every piece, and now it's ruined. Weinstein doesn't think I should dock his wages for it. And he thinks I should pay him for working today if he leaves to take the girl to a doctor."

Emily could hardly believe her ears. Mr. Meyer expected

a penniless employee to pay for an accident that wasn't his fault? And now he was going to be docked for taking his daughter to the hospital? "If you'll give me the taxi money," she told the owner, "I'll take Ruth to the hospital."

Mr. Meyer removed a small purse from his pocket, unsnapped it, and counted out a few coins. "Here."

Emily studied the money in her palm. "That may not be enough to get there," she said.

Scowling, Mr. Meyer reached for another coin. "I hope I can trust you to see to it that I get any change back."

That did it. Emily opened her mouth to scream at this man, to remind him about the money he owed Cousin Lucretia's father. But before she got the words out, Maggie interrupted. "I'll take her to the hospital. I can do it faster than you can with Sarah and Robert."

Emily considered her options. Maggie couldn't afford to lose a day's wages either, but speed was what mattered for Ruth, and it was true that Sarah and Robert would slow Emily down. She studied the coins in her palm and handed them over to Maggie.

Maggie glared at Mr. Meyer. "I'll be off then. Come with me, Ruth love." Mr. Weinstein stood up, tears rolling down his cheeks. He whispered a few words to Ruth and patted her on the shoulder before she headed out the door with Maggie.

Mr. Weinstein's hands were shaking. He was in no condition to operate the dangerous cutting machine right now, but Emily couldn't think of anything to say to him, even if he understood English. She offered him a hopeful smile, but she didn't feel a bit hopeful as she swept her little brother into her arms and carried him down the stairs.

On their way to the exit, they passed Ruth's stool and the chair next to it where Maggie had been sitting.

Robert pointed. "Look! Maggie's lunch pail. She forgot!" he sang. "Plumb forgot! Plumb forgot! Plumb forgot!"

CHAPTER FOURTEEN

Baltimore, Maryland
May 19, 1912

Dear Albert,

Our sermon in church this morning was on repentance, and I
could hardly sit still knowing that I had said something that made
you cross. I don't know what I wrote that upset you, but I want
you to know I'm sorry. For whatever it was. Please forgive me.

I hope you didn't mean it when you said you weren't going to
write to me anymore. Even if you did, though, I still want to write
to you, especially about the "Titanic."

I thought I was through having bad dreams about the ship, but
I had the worst one of my whole life last night, and I woke up
shaking. You'll probably think I'm silly for being so scared. But
here goes. I was sitting in a "Titanic" lifeboat, and people all
around me in the water were thrashing and screaming. One of the
people in the water was so covered with blood that I couldn't see
his face, but I knew it was you. You held out your hand for me to

grab it, but the officer on our boat ordered people at the oars to row in the other direction.

Then in my dream it was the next morning and I was on the deck of the "Carpathia" looking for you. I looked and looked but I couldn't find you anywhere, so I started to cry. Then a voice said, "It's your fault he died, because you didn't rescue him."

That's the worst dream I can possibly imagine.

I'm sure one of the reasons I had the dream is that I knew you were angry with me. Another reason is that I had such a terrible day yesterday. Remember when I told you about Ruth Weinstein, the little girl who works in the garment factory with Maggie? I went to Meyer's (that's the owner of the factory) to take Maggie her lunch yesterday, and while I was there, Ruth cut off her whole thumb in one of the machines. (Imagine!) Next to the "Titanic," it was the worst accident I had ever seen. Blood spilled everywhere, and poor Ruth will have difficulty all her life trying to manage without the thumb of her right hand.

The wicked man she works for didn't even seem to care. The only thing he worried about was getting paid for the fabric stained by her blood. I was so mad! The accident was all Mr. Meyer's fault for not keeping the place cleaner. (A rat startled her and she fell onto the table where her father was operating a cutting machine.) Nobody should have to work in a factory that filthy. I wish I had a thousand dollars. I'd buy that horrible place and then burn it down.

Anyway, Ruth's accident has made me think about the thing that Mama keeps telling me. She says the best way for me to forget about the "Titanic" and all the people who died on it is to get busy doing things that will help people who are still alive. The person I would like to help is poor little nine-year-old Ruth

Weinstein. Something needs to be done for her. I haven't figured out what it is yet, but I'll think of something. And then I'll do it.

How is Ginny getting along with her scarlet fever? Sarah's quarantine sign is down. I took her with me to the factory yesterday, but the sickening odor and the sight of blood made her vomit. She's feeling all right today, but Mama has decided not to enroll her in school this year. It's too near the end of the school year for her to start, so she won't begin first grade until next fall. For now Mama has decided to take Sarah and Robert with her to Brewer House. There, Sarah will help Mama watch Robert until I get out of school each day.

Minding Sarah and Robert means I don't have time to play. I see Louise Kezerian only at school (or walking home afterward). I don't see Maggie until she gets home from work, which is pretty late, usually.

Mama and Cousin Lucretia are just about through scrubbing and papering Brewer House, but they're busy doing other things. Cousin Lucretia is still raising money from all the rich people she knows in Baltimore, and Mama is finding volunteers to teach the classes they're planning.

Sincerely,
Emily

P.S. I'm sorry you don't want to hear about Louise Kezerian's birthday party. I was going to tell you about it, but now I guess I won't.

P.P.S. I hope you still like to draw the way you used to. You're a very good artist.

CHAPTER FIFTEEN

Emily couldn't concentrate.

In her seat next to Irene Clayton she had read the beginning paragraphs about Andrew Jackson's presidency three times, but she didn't know any more about the crises that he had faced in the White House than she had understood fifteen minutes earlier. She had had another nightmare about the *Titanic* the previous night, but instead of dreaming about people who had actually fallen off the real ship, she dreamed that she was trying to save Maggie Flanagan and Ruth Weinstein from the icy water.

When she woke up shaking and perspiring in the middle of the night, she was relieved to hear Maggie's soft, furry snoring as she lay asleep beside her in bed. But once awake, Emily tossed and turned with worry until dawn. She worried about Maggie, who had to work in that foul-smelling and dangerous sweatshop of Otto Meyer's. She worried about Ruth, who would have to go through life without her right thumb. And she worried about Albert, who had misunderstood a letter she'd sent him and would probably never write to her again.

"You may close your books, boys and girls," announced the teacher. "Louise Kezerian has had a death in her family and is leaving today for Pittsburgh. But before she goes, she has something she'd like to say to you."

All eyes turned to Louise. Emily wondered who in her friend's family had died.

"Well—" she began.

"No, no, Louise. Come stand in front."

Louise hesitated for a moment before putting both hands flat on her desk to push herself to her feet. She lumbered to the front of the room in her flat-footed way.

"Well—" she repeated. "About my birthday party—"

Emily's stomach fluttered. Why was she so nervous? she wondered. She already knew the details of Louise's upcoming party and had decided four days ago, when Albert's letter had arrived, that she wouldn't go. She just hadn't had the opportunity yet to tell Louise.

"Uh—you all know my birthday is—uh—on June eighth," Louise continued.

For a girl who had no trouble telling Emily all her secrets on their walks home from school, Louise was strangely tongue-tied. Even so, everyone seemed to be listening attentively. Across the aisle from Emily, Royal Ludlow stopped folding a paper airplane and leaned forward in his seat. Next to Emily, Irene Clayton crossed the fingers on both hands.

"The party's going to be at Gwynn Oak Park."

Small gasps of pleasure erupted around the room as

Emily doubled over at her desk, pressing her hands tight against her stomach. Why did her insides feel so skittish just because she was going to miss a silly party? She didn't need to ride in a goat cart. (Louise had told her how awful they smelled.) Or a roller coaster. (She'd bet they were dangerous. What if one of the cars ran off the track or got stuck at the top?) Or a rowboat. (Even the thought of getting anywhere near a boat was enough to send shivers down her back.)

"Father says I can ask as many people as I want this year. So all of you are invited."

In the seat next to Emily's, Irene Clayton uncrossed her fingers. Excitement bubbled around the room until it came to full boil. *"Silence, boys and girls!"* yelled Miss Cameron as she pounded her desk with a ruler. *"Silence!"*

As the chattering died down, Louise sucked in her cheeks and looked anxiously in Royal Ludlow's direction before turning her eyes away. Emily knew what was coming. For some reason her stomach felt as if it were slowly stretching and then bending its ends together, like the vinegar taffy she sometimes pulled for Sarah and Robert.

Louise wiped sweaty hands on the sides of her starched cotton dress. "Mother says that since I'll be thirteen on my birthday—only a year away from high school—it's time I practiced party manners, like Miss Cameron teaches." She nodded anxiously toward the teacher, and Miss Cameron smiled back. "Mother says all of us should practice acting like grown-ups somewhere besides our dancing lessons at school. Mother says we should come to my birthday party in pairs. Boy-girl pairs."

Poor Louise, Emily thought. She pretends to be so tough,

but no one realizes how shy and lonely she really is. Emily knew for a fact that Louise had dreamed up the pairs idea herself, just to be able to spend the whole day with Royal Ludlow.

"Mother decided that we could stay at Gwynn Oak Park all day until ten o'clock so we can dance to Charles Farson's orchestra in the evening," Louise continued.

That was another fib, Emily knew. Louise's mother had had to be wheedled and wheedled to agree to a party that lasted as late as ten o'clock. But the whole reason for holding the party at Gwynn Oak was that Louise knew about the orchestra there, and she was determined that the party wouldn't end before the dancing began.

"What about the rides?" a boy called out.

"Yeah, what about the roller coaster?" said someone else.

Except for Louise herself, everyone in the class seemed more interested in the rides at Gwynn Oak Park than in choosing partners or dancing in the evening. Emily wondered what Royal Ludlow would think if he knew that this whole scheme had been planned just for him.

"We'll go on the rides all afternoon," Louise explained. "We'll meet at the hot-dog stand at two o'clock, and I'll stamp all of you on your hands so the concessionaires will let you go on the rides as often as you want."

"Even the roller coaster?"

Louise nodded. "Father has arranged for all the rides. But you have to come to the party in pairs. Every girl has to invite a boy to be her partner."

"There aren't enough boys to go around," Irene Clayton

whined. "There used to be two extra girls," she added, giving Emily a dirty look, "but now there are three."

"So three girls will have to invite boys who aren't in our class," Louise explained. "You can invite someone in our class or someone from any other room at school. You can even invite someone from a different school." She nodded toward her friend. "Emily's going to ask a boy she met on the *Titanic*. He lives all the way in Virginia."

Emily shook her head, hoping to interrupt Louise's explanation. She hadn't had a chance to tell Louise about Albert's letter. She hoped to get Louise's attention to mouth the message that Albert wouldn't be coming, but Louise didn't look her way.

Just then the front door of the classroom opened, and a tall man carrying a cane and a black derby walked stiffly into the room toward Louise. He put a gloved hand on the girl's shoulder in a manner that indicated he must be her father and spoke quietly to her and Miss Cameron. Except for some of the first-class passengers Emily had seen at the church service on the *Titanic*, she had never encountered such a dignified gentleman before.

Emily leaned toward her seatmate. "Is that Louise's father?"

Irene nodded. "Uh-huh."

He was wearing a black pin-striped suit that was immaculately tailored, and his handlebar mustache curled gracefully at the edges. Mr. Kezerian probably went to a barbershop every day. He was nothing like scraggly old Otto Meyer.

Of course! Emily wondered why she hadn't thought of

it before. Maggie should be working for Louise's father, not Otto Meyer. His canneries would surely be more pleasant than Mr. Meyer's disgusting and dangerous sweatshop. And Louise could help Maggie find a job at one of them.

In the front of the room, Louise, who was gesturing wildly, seemed to be arguing with her father. He removed a pocket watch from his vest pocket and held it up for her to see. Then, taking her by the arm, he tried to urge her toward the door.

Louise would have none of it. She broke away from him to address the class. "Father says we have to leave for Pittsburgh now. Don't any girls invite any boys until I get back to Baltimore on Friday. I have to make a list with all your names before you do any inviting so the pairs all work out right. Every boy will get just one invitation. I want this to be fair. See?"

Mr. Kezerian took her arm again. "Come on, Louise."

As he led the girl toward the open door, a babble of voices carried throughout the room, but Irene Clayton shouted above the noise. "What about Emily? You said she had already decided what boy she was going to invite."

"No! I may not ask him," Emily called out. She assumed she had spoken loud enough for everyone to hear, but Louise obviously didn't.

"Emily's friend doesn't matter because he's not in our class. Except for her, don't any of you girls invite a partner until I get back. None of you," Louise ordered as her father whisked her through the doorway.

The buzzing in the room became a roar.

"*Silence!*" yelled Miss Cameron as she whacked her desk with her ruler. She whacked it again. "*Silence!* That's better. I know you're all excited about Louise's party, but we have work to do. All of you turn back again to the lesson about Andrew Jackson and find the place where you were reading."

Emily opened her book again, but she had so many new things to worry about that she had even more trouble concentrating now than she'd had before. How would Louise feel when Emily told her that she didn't want to go to the party? Would Louise be so hurt or angry that she wouldn't help Maggie get a job at one of her father's canneries?

When the recess bell rang, Emily stood to join the line that was forming at the side of the room. But before she got there, a new worry, as bad as all the others put together, hit her. Royal Ludlow slipped her a note:

Don't ask that guy in Virginia. I'll go to Louise's party with you.

CHAPTER SIXTEEN

Emily quickly folded Royal's note and hid it in her pocket as she stood in the line at the back of the room. There was a rule against passing notes in class, and Miss Cameron embarrassed students who wrote them by reading them aloud for everyone to hear. Emily didn't want anyone to know about her note from Royal. She didn't want to go to Louise's party with him, even if Louise would permit it, which of course she wouldn't.

Emily wished she had never heard of Gwynn Oak Park. She wished she had never come to this school. She wished Mama would let her study at home every day. Most of all, she wished that Albert weren't mad at her. She had tried a million times to remember what she had said in her letter that might have upset him. Did he think her new friends were more important to her than he was?

At last Miss Cameron signaled her pupils to leave for recess. Behind Irene Clayton, Emily marched single file with all her classmates—through the hall, downstairs to the first floor, through the outside door, and down the final steps to the playground.

Irene turned around to face Emily, her smile the size of a banana. "Didn't I tell you that Louise gives the best parties in the whole world? And this year everyone gets to go. Won't it be fun? I've never been on a roller coaster before, have you?"

Emily had to admit she hadn't. She had seen pictures of roller coasters, but never a real one. The one at Gwynn Oak Park, she knew, had been installed in 1909, after her family had left for Ceylon. She didn't think there were any roller coasters in Ceylon, or India either, probably.

"I've been to Gwynn Oak Park, though," Irene continued. "Oh, it's so beautiful. Pretty paths through the trees—more trees than you've ever seen in one spot—and a beautiful lake where people go boating. Last year we went there for a picnic and watched the boaters while we ate. Mama fixed a wonderful lunch with tomato sandwiches, and for dessert we had apricots she'd pinched from the cannery."

Emily stared at the other girl. Did *pinched* mean what she thought it did, that her mother had stolen the fruit? Was Irene really as proud of that as she sounded?

"I love apricots, don't you?" Irene asked.

Emily nodded. "About the cannery—"

"We couldn't go on the roller coaster, though," Irene said. "The trolley costs five cents each way. That's a total of sixty cents for our family, so Papa didn't have another sixty to let us go on any rides. But he bought a bag of popcorn that all us children shared. I'm so excited about Louise's party, aren't you? Do you think she might buy each of us our own bag of popcorn? Mr. Kezerian could afford that maybe, rich as he is."

Irene was straying from the subject again. "You told me once that your mama works at Mr. Kezerian's cannery," Emily said.

"Uh-huh." Irene pulled a drawstring bag made from a faded cotton print from the pocket of her apron. "Want to play jacks?"

Emily nodded. She wasn't very good at jacks because Louise thought the game was only for sissies, and they had only played once or twice. But Emily didn't want to barge into a game of marbles with a group of boys when Louise wasn't here to do the barging.

"Mr. Kezerian is so handsome-looking," said Emily. "I'll bet his cannery is a wonderful place to work."

"Well, it's no worse than any other cannery, I guess."

Irene led the way to a place on the concrete that wasn't occupied and motioned for Emily to sit down.

"Doesn't your mother like working there?" Emily wanted to know.

"She likes having a little extra. For food, you know," Irene explained as she took the ball and jacks from her bag. "Papa's wages digging cellars don't buy much food for a family big as ours. Wintertime, we mostly just eat potatoes and cabbage. Turnips sometimes. On days when Mama gets paid, she'll maybe stop at the bakery and bring home a sweet bun or two. She cuts them up so all of us can have a bite." She handed the ball and jacks to Emily. "Here, toss them to see who goes first."

Emily accepted the metal jacks. With palms up and together, she tossed them into the air, caught them on the backs of her hands, and tossed them up again to catch them in her palms. She dropped four out of the ten. Then she scooped them all up and handed the star-shaped toys over so Irene could take her turn at tossing. Irene dropped only one, so she began the game.

"But about the cannery?" Emily said. "I have a friend who might be looking for a new job. Would she like it at Mr. Kezerian's cannery?"

An experienced jacks player, Irene had no trouble playing the game and talking at the same time. "I don't guess anyone likes working anywhere. They do it because they has to is the way I figure things. Mama takes the baby with her. Keeps Nora in a box by her feet. Lots of mamas take their little ones. Older children too. Ones about eight or nine can help with the work sometimes."

"There are laws in this state against child labor," said Emily. She knew that for a fact. When she had told Cousin Lucretia about poor Ruth's injury, Papa's cousin had seemed mad enough to pop. Cousin Lucretia was one of the ladies who had gone personally to the State Capitol in Annapolis to lobby for stricter legislation about child labor.

"Yes," said Irene, "but Joseph Kezerian don't worry about little things like laws. The inspectors don't pay too much mind either as far as Mama can tell. Wouldn't be surprised if Louise's wonderful daddy didn't slip the inspectors a little something now and then."

"You mean bribery! Louise's father wouldn't do that!"

"I didn't say he would. I just said it might could happen. Anything is possible, you know."

Emily nodded, even though she didn't agree with Irene. She was sure that Mr. Kezerian would never stoop to bribery.

"Maybe the inspectors don't care about the laws because the work season don't last very long," Irene continued. "Some canneries are open only two or three months in the summer, but Mama likes Kezerian's because it sometimes goes six. They're doing spinach now. Then come strawberries and peas and beans. Peaches and tomatoes come in September. Children who work in the canneries start school in October, usually. Mama says the teachers understand. Have to, I guess. Can your friend who wants a job read and write and figure? In English, I mean."

"Well. A little. She went to school in Ireland, but not for very long."

"I'm the only one in our family can read and write and figure, so I don't plan to work in no cannery when I graduate after eighth grade next year. I plan to get me a real job, all year round. Selling at the five-and-dime, maybe. I'm real lucky to stay in school as long as eighth grade, but Mama and Papa wanted me to get an education so I can get a good job when I graduate. That way I can help the family more."

Emily accepted the jacks from Irene, who had gotten all the way to sevensies without making a mistake. She hesitated before she began her turn. "Is Kezerian's hiring right now?"

Irene shrugged. "Maybe. Couldn't rightly say. Tell your

friend if she wants a job, she should wear rubber boots or stout shoes."

"Why's that?" Emily tossed the jacks to the ground. Then she threw the ball into the air with her right hand, picked up a single jack with the same hand to place in her left palm, and caught the ball again with her right.

"Muck. The floors are covered with it. Peach pits. Tomato pulp. Apricot peelings. Depends on the season, I guess, but there's always slop and muck."

Emily looked up openmouthed at Irene, so startled by the new accusation that she dropped the ball she had just thrown in the air. How could Irene sit there telling one wicked fib after another? Did she really expect Emily to believe such terrible tales? Irene was undoubtedly making up stories about Mr. Kezerian because she didn't like Louise. Emily felt she should defend her friend but was too angry to know how to begin.

She scooped up the jacks and ball and handed them to Irene. "Here."

If Irene sensed that Emily was angry, she didn't let on. "Slop and muck," she repeated. "Some of the women go barefoot, but Mama won't. Too many mice running around."

That did it. Emily was sure Irene's whole description of Kezerian's cannery was nothing but a lie. "I saw how Mr. Kezerian was dressed," Emily said hotly. "He wouldn't wear fancy clothes like that with garbage on the floor."

Irene shrugged. "Believe what you want. Your friend who's looking for a job will tell you about Kezerian's if she decides to work there."

"Canneries—of all places—have to be kept clean. People eat the food that comes out of them. And I'm sure Mr. Kezerian doesn't let mice run around his factory," said Emily.

"Well, he don't keep things clean. He don't do lots of things he should. I can't believe you want to be friends with Louise Kezerian."

"I like Louise. And I don't think it's nice for people to pretend to be her friend just because they want to be invited to her party."

"Why not? Why shouldn't I go to Gwynn Oak Park and ride on the roller coaster for once? It's the least Mr. Kezerian can do for our family when he makes Mama work seventy hours a week for wages that are hardly big enough to buy two or three sweet buns once in a while."

"But you shouldn't be nice to someone just so they'll invite you to a party. It's—it's hypocritical."

"Listen here, Emily Brewer. You may get better marks on your spelling tests than I do, but you don't know nothing about this world. Nothing. Rich people take advantage of poor ones every single day of the year. So if we can turn the tables on them just once, I say good for us. Right now you might say you like Louise, but that's just because you don't know her very well yet. You'll find out about her and her family. Just wait and see."

CHAPTER SEVENTEEN

After school Emily walked alone to Brewer House to relieve Mama of the care of her little sister and brother. Sarah was outdoors on the sidewalk, pulling Robert in an old wooden wagon that Cousin Lucretia had found somewhere. More surprisingly, Maggie was outside the building on her hands and knees, scrubbing the four marble steps that led to the front door. Emily knew that all the ladies in this part of Baltimore scrubbed their front steps every day, but she couldn't imagine why Maggie would be doing it at Brewer House rather than at home, and at a time when she should have been at Meyer's sweatshop.

"How did you get here?" Emily demanded. "Why aren't you at work?"

"Otto Meyer let me go, he did. Or maybe you could say I let meself go. Whatever way you put it, I'm not working for that shameful old skinflint no more."

"What happened?"

Maggie stood up, rubbing her back as if it was sore. "I've

been sewing me fingers to bare bones in that filthy pigsty he calls a factory, with nary a soul to speak to and fretting over poor little Ruth and what her family was going to do without the few pennies she earns each day. So, at lunchtime I made it a point to go straight upstairs to talk to his highness Mr. Otto Meyer. I told him exactly what I thought of someone who was no more concerned about a little nine-year-old girl losing a thumb in his varmint-filled sweatshop than to make her papa pay for the damage to a few miserable pieces of cloth."

"Oh, Maggie! You didn't really!" Emily exclaimed.

"Well, maybe not in the exact same words I'm using here with you. But I made it plain, I did, how I felt. So he made it plain how he felt too. Told me I was an impertinent piece of baggage who had no right talking to an employer about how to run his business and that at least fifty girls on the street would be happy to have me place. So I told him I was just as happy to give it to them, and good riddance. So here I am, scrubbing the steps of Brewer House and beholden to Miss Lucretia for the nickel I'll be getting for me efforts today, and the next nickel I'll be earning tomorrow for scrubbing here again."

Emily hesitated, wondering how to say what she was thinking without hurting her friend's feelings. This was the second job Maggie had lost in less than a month, and it didn't seem very responsible for her to quit the sweatshop before she had found another job. Did she expect to let Emily's mother and cousin support her forever? Emily rolled her tongue around her lips before speaking. "How will you save enough money to bring your family to America when you're earning just five cents a day?"

"Well, I guess I haven't mentioned me good news, now have I? Me mum always said that there's never a devil bringing a body mischief without an angel hiding right behind the door."

"An angel?" asked Emily. "You mean Cousin Lucretia?"

"Well, Miss Lucretia is an angel, all right, but not the exact one I was referring to today. No, me angel today is our landlady, Missus Lieberman."

"What did she do?"

"Remember when Miss Lucretia said the best garment factory in Baltimore was owned by a man named Herman Bamberger?"

Emily nodded.

"Well, I went home from Meyer's sweatshop this afternoon feeling foolish and sore as a dog that's tried to wrestle a porcupine. Missus Lieberman saw me in the hall and wanted to know about me long face. When I told her everything that had happened at Meyer's, she said she had a brother-in-law who owned a garment factory and she'd be telling him about me at synagogue this weekend. You'll never guess his name."

"Not Herman Bamberger?"

"One and the same."

"Oh, Maggie!" Emily hugged her friend as dirty water from Maggie's brush dripped on both their skirts.

Maggie took a deep breath and continued her story. "So then I came to Brewer House to tell your mama and Miss

Lucretia me good news and offer to mind Sarah and Robert till you got here from school. I also told them I was aching to go see how me poor little love of a Ruth is getting along without the use of her thumb, but didn't have the two nickels I'd need to pay for me trolley fare. That's when Miss Lucretia offered to pay me for this scrubbing job."

"I'm surprised she didn't give you the money to go see Ruth," Emily said. "She was as upset as you and I were about Ruth's accident. She hates employers who hire children because they're cheap labor."

"No, she don't care much for flimflam artists that calls themselves factory owners. Working for pay was my idea. Miss Lucretia offered to drive me to Ruth's house in her nice Packard, but I could see she was in the middle of adding a big stack of figures and didn't need to be interrupted. Anyway, I've taken enough charity from your family and need to do a bit to pay back some of it."

That statement relieved Emily's mind somewhat. "Can you find your way to Ruth's house on the trolley?" she asked. "How do you know where she lives?"

"I asked her papa."

"But I thought he doesn't speak English."

"No, but Otto Meyer helped me that much at least. He asked Mr. Weinstein and then wrote the address down for me on a bit of paper. See?" She withdrew it from a pocket. "Miss Lucretia told me how to find the place and which trolley I should take. So I'm going there first thing tomorrow morning. Soon as I earn another nickel for scrubbing."

"I want to go with you," Emily said. "Don't go in the morning. Wait until my school is out."

Maggie poured her dirty water into the gutter. "I'd like that right enough, but your mama might not. She expects you to get here straight from school to mind Sarah and Robert for her."

"We can take them with us," Emily said.

"EE-YOO! Blood!" said Sarah, who had parked the wagon near enough to Maggie and Emily to overhear their conversation.

"Blood? Where?" said Emily.

"At Ruth's house. Like at the factory when she hurt her thumb."

"There won't be any blood," said Maggie. "The doctor sewed her thumb up."

Sarah seemed shocked. "You don't sew *people's thumbs!*"

"Doctors do," said Maggie. "That's how they stop more blood from coming. Then they put bandages on the wounds, all nice and clean like."

"Cross your heart?" said Sarah.

"Cross me heart," said Maggie, making the gesture with her hand.

"Wel-l-l-l," said Sarah. "Maybe I'll go."

Robert grinned. "Me too."

Maggie turned to face Emily. "You'll be needing a few nickels of your own to take the three of you on the trolley. But you may not be worried about taking more charity from Miss Lucretia, you being family and all."

"Mama and I have taken more from Cousin Lucretia

than you have," Emily said. "If you work for the trolley fare, I should too. Robert probably doesn't have to pay, so it will just be four nickels for Sarah and me. I'll ask Cousin Lucretia if she'll let me start scrubbing those steps the day after tomorrow, after you've had a turn. I'm as anxious as you are to see how Ruth is doing. Please take me with you."

"I will if Miss Lucretia will pay you in advance so we can go tomorrow for sure."

"I'll go ask her right now," Emily said, running up the steps.

CHAPTER EIGHTEEN

Through the open window Emily could see the motorman, his face red with frustration. "Dagnab it," he muttered.

"Dagnab it," echoed Robert. Holding Emily's shoulder for support, he jumped up and down on the rattan seat of the stalled trolley car. "Dagnab it, dagnab it, dagnab it."

"Hush, Robert," she said. "That isn't a nice way to talk."

Robert pointed out the window. "He said it."

"Never mind. Don't you talk that way. And sit down, please. You're hurting me."

Robert sat, grinning at Maggie. They were looking directly at each other because Maggie had slid the back of the seat on which she was sitting with Sarah to face the wrong direction. Sliding the backs of trolley seats was a trick she had learned from her papa, she explained. He had watched the motormen do it at the ends of the trolley lines because the cars themselves couldn't turn around on their tracks.

Facing her sister, Emily could see that Sarah's lips were

pinched into a knot, the way Miss Cameron's sometimes were. In her mind, Emily imagined Sarah standing at the front of a classroom, holding a pair of pince-nez in one hand and pounding her desk with the other. *"Silence!"* she was shouting. *"Silence!"*

Right that minute, however, Sarah spoke softly. *"Dagnab it* is slang, isn't it, Emily?"

Emily nodded. "Yes."

Sarah smoothed her dress over her knees. "Mama says we mustn't use slang, doesn't she?"

Emily nodded again.

"I do!" shrieked Robert. "Dagnab it!" He swung his legs back and forth.

Maggie leaned across her lap to the other seat and gave Robert a hug. "Yer a disgrace to the right proper Brewer family, you are, but us Flanagans don't mind a yappy little fellow like you once in a while. Fact is, you make me right homesick for me own little Denny. He was just about your size, not too much bigger, when I left home."

Outside the trolley the motorman was stuffing his work gloves into his pockets. Emily watched as he trudged to the open door, clomped up the steps of the trolley, and addressed the few passengers still sitting in their seats. The car was near the end of its line, and most of the people on board had already exited. "I can't get the trolley back on its wire, so I guess we're stuck here until someone notices that the car is missing and sends a rescue team for the dad-blamed thing."

"Oooh," wailed a heavy-set woman across the aisle who was dressed all in black.

"'Blamed thing," said Robert.

"Robert is using slang again, Emily," Sarah tattled. "Make him stop."

"Hush, Robert," Emily whispered.

"Anyone what wants to can get off," said the motorman. "Otherwise you'll just have to sit here and wait with me, I reckon."

"How long will that be?" called a gentleman sitting in back.

"Can't rightly say for sure. Couple hours, maybe. The office has one of those tellyphone things," the motorman reported, "but how do they expect us to call in from a place like this? Who around this fiddle-faddle neighborhood is likely to own a millionaire gimcrack like a tellyphone?"

"Are we millionaires?" Sarah whispered to her sister.

"Of course not," said Emily.

"But we have a telephone," Sarah argued. "It's nailed right to the wall in the kitchen. Mama uses it all the time."

Emily replied with a nod of agreement. "Shh," she said.

"Can't you do anything?" the lady across the aisle grumbled to the motorman. "I need to help my daughter-in-law prepare the Sabbath."

"'Fraid not, ma'am. Not 'less you know where I can find me a goldurn tellyphone contraption around these parts. It takes two tellyphones to send a message to anyone, you know."

For the first time, Emily studied the houses through her trolley window. They were made of wood, not brick, and they weren't attached to each other like the row houses closer to town. The walks in front of them were dirt paths, not paved sidewalks, and she was pretty sure none of the residents bothered to scrub their front steps.

"Well, I don't know about anyone else," said the lady who was worried about her Sabbath preparations, "but I'm getting off. I'll feel more useful walking to my son's house than sitting here." She elbowed the motorman out of the way and clomped down the steps.

The gentleman who was sitting in back and a young couple near him followed her up the aisle. The Brewers and Maggie were the only passengers still sitting.

Maggie stood up. "We might as well hoof it too. Ruth's house shouldn't be more than a half mile from here. We can take turns carrying Robert if we have to. I'll take the first turn if you like."

"I don't need carrying. I'm big," he announced, but he accepted Maggie's help down the steps, and he had trotted past only a few houses before he raised both arms to her, gesturing to be boosted up.

Maggie bent over to lift him. "You are big, you are! I could break me back lifting such a tub of lard. What say you carry me on the next block?"

"No! Let Emily carry me! Make her take turns!"

Emily and Maggie both giggled at that, but not Sarah. "Robert always gets to be carried," she muttered, her chin almost touching her chest.

Robert waved to two boys who had dug holes in the dirt and were playing a game of potsies with their marbles. Farther along, they passed a man smoking a cigarette on his front steps.

Sarah tugged at Emily's sleeve. "The trolley man was wrong," she whispered. "There's a millionaire."

"What makes you say that?" Emily asked.

"He doesn't have to go to work. He just sits there."

"Maybe he's been let go, like me," suggested Maggie.

"Don't worry. You'll have a job next week," Emily promised. "If Mrs. Lieberman can't help you with her brother-in-law, I know my friend Louise will help you find work at her father's cannery."

Sarah tugged Emily's sleeve again. "What's that awful smell?"

Maggie took a whiff. "Outdoor jakes, I'd be guessing," she said.

"What are jakes?" asked Sarah.

"Privies, you'd call them," Maggie explained. She turned to Emily. "Are you Brewers such royalty that you've always lived in houses with indoor plumbing? I never saw a real water closet in me life until I got on the ship to America. Of course the high-and-mighty Mrs. Huffaker had a regular collection of them in her castle of a house. Three water closets, they were, which I was privileged to scour every day. Or sometimes twice a day if she didn't think I'd done it right the first go-around."

"Sarah should know what privies are. We used them in Ceylon," Emily said. "And we used chamber pots on all the tramp steamers we took before the *Titanic*. But we changed ships so often around the coasts of Africa that it took nearly two months to get from Ceylon to England. She may have forgotten what it was like in Ceylon."

"I have not," said Sarah.

"Well, my nose has gone right botchedy if those aren't outdoor jakes we're smelling," Maggie said. "Didn't someone tell me that Baltimore was getting so high-flown, it was putting sewer lines all over the city?"

"Look!" Pointing, Robert struggled to be free of Maggie's grasp. "Ruth!" he cried when he reached the ground. "Ruth!" He toddled off toward a group of three children sitting in the dirt about thirty yards away.

As Emily and the others followed Robert toward the children sitting on the ground, she could see that they were making mud pies in discarded tin cans, using water from a rusty pail and old sticks for stirring. Ruth's bandage, just a few days after her trip to the hospital, was caked with filth. Emily wondered if the doctor hadn't warned her about keeping it clean.

"Ruth, love," exclaimed Maggie. "How are you? I've been worrying meself silly about you."

Ruth stood up to return Maggie's hug. "All right, I guess. I don't know what Papa will do without the pennies I earn, but I'm learning to use my left hand." Her face brightened as she nodded to her friends. "Me and Esther and Nathan are going to have a mud-pie fair."

"Want to buy one?" said Esther, who was about Ruth's age or a little younger. Emily tried not to gasp when she saw the girl's mangled right hand. The fingers looked as if their bones had once been crushed and broken.

Emily leaned down and took Esther by the wrist. "What happened to you?"

Esther pulled her hand away, hiding it behind her back. "Don't remember," she said, staring glumly at her mud pie.

"Esther fainted," Ruth reported.

"Esther and her ma both fainted," said Nathan. "Women always faint."

"Why did you faint?" Maggie asked the girl. "Where were you?"

Esther studied her tin can full of mud without speaking, so Ruth answered for her again. "They were sorting peas at the cannery. Esther got her hand caught in the belt or something. I don't know exactly."

There seemed to be a pattern in these accidents that Emily didn't like. She looked from Esther back to Ruth. "What was she doing at the cannery? She wasn't working, was she? She's not even as big as you are."

"Mamas at the cannery always take their children along. Some work—the big ones anyway. Some don't."

Esther looked up from her mud pie. "I worked," she said.

Maggie and Emily exchanged a worried look. "How old are you?" Emily asked.

"Don't know," said the girl, casting her eyes down again.

Emily was horrified. This girl didn't even know how old she was, yet her mother—and the awful factory owner, whoever he was—let her work around dangerous machinery in the cannery.

"Esther's mama thought she was big enough to earn some pennies," Ruth explained. "Their family needed money real bad, so she let Esther stand in line by the grown-ups and try to help. Esther saw a rotten pea or rock or something going along on the belt and followed it to get it off. But she was too little to do it right, I guess."

The sight of Esther's twisted hand sent shivers down Emily's back. "That sounds terrible. I don't blame you for fainting," she told the girl.

"I didn't faint, and I was hurt worse," said Nathan. He was older than the girls, probably eleven or twelve. He seemed to be hiding his left hand in his knickers pocket, but when he held up his arm, Emily could see that it ended in a stump.

"Good heavens!" said Emily.

"Blessed mother of Jesus!" cried Maggie. "How did you lose your hand?"

"I didn't lose it. Doctor chopped it off."

Sarah's eyes were the size of golf balls. "How come?"

"Gangrene, doctor said. My hand turned all smelly and black. So he chopped it off. I told Ruth that will happen to her if she keeps getting her bandage dirty, but she never listens."

"No it won't. My mama says that can't happen. My mama says you're full of scary *yatatata*," Ruth reported.

"No, Ruth, Nathan is right. You should—" Emily began.

"Yeah," Nathan interrupted. "What does her old lady know? Ruth's ma just sits in her bed all day coughing and coughing. My ma pays her a nickel a day to mind me and feed me supper, but all I ever get to eat is stuff I bring from home. Bread or a raw potato maybe. Ain't that right, Esther?"

Esther didn't look up. "Yes," she whispered.

"I guess I know more about gangrene than someone who just sits in bed coughing all the time. Little sores turn into big ones, and then they get all smelly and black if you don't watch out. I didn't even cut my finger all the way off like Ruth did, but look what happened to me." He held up his stump again.

"How did you hurt yourself?" Emily asked.

"Shuckin' oysters at the fish cannery. Little kids like Ruth and Esther here can't do it, just big strong ones. You have to push and twist at the same time with all your might or the shells won't come open. And you use real sharp knives. My knife slipped."

"I've been cut before." Sarah studied her own hands. "The doctor never chopped my hands off."

"Well, don't ever use a dirty bandage," Nathan warned. "I just found an old rag at the cannery and wrapped it around my finger so I could go on working that day, but I ended up without a hand."

Maggie seemed strangely subdued. Emily suspected that the sight of these injured children reminded her of a letter she had just received from her mother in Ireland. With no father to support them, and her oldest daughter in America, Maggie's mother was taking in washing. In the past month there had been two accidents with the equipment. Maggie's seven-year-old brother had burned his hand while tending the stove used for boiling the laundry, and her nine-year-old sister had burned hers on the flatiron.

"It breaks my heart, it does, all this suffering of little tykes," Maggie said. "Aren't there any children living in this neighborhood who still have all the blessed fingers and hands the good Lord gave them?"

For once Esther spoke up, nodding toward the boy. "Nathan's brothers. All of them."

"Yep," Nathan agreed. "They ain't been hurt. Not yet."

Not yet! Emily repeated to herself. Did all the children around here assume they would be injured at some job sooner or later? She hardly dared to ask Nathan the next question. "Do your brothers shuck oysters?"

"Yep," he said.

"There are laws against child labor in this state!" Emily's voice was shrill. "Cousin Lucretia and her friends worked hard to get them passed." She turned to the children. "Your employers should all be reported."

"Where were you working?" Maggie asked Nathan. "What's the name of it?"

"Seaside Fish Cannery."

"How about you?" she asked Esther.

Esther didn't answer or even look up, so Ruth answered for her. "At 'Zerian's, I think."

Emily's heart skipped. "You don't mean Kezerian's, do you?"

"Yes. That's it. Kezerian's," said Ruth.

Emily swallowed. "Kezerian's is the cannery where I hoped to get you a job," she told Maggie. "I was going to ask my friend Louise Kezerian to help you. I can't believe her father would break the law to let children as young as Esther work for him. That's sinful!"

Robert, whom everyone had ignored, was stirring a sloppy mixture of mud in a tin can. "Sinful," he muttered.

"These poor darlings," wailed Maggie. "These poor, poor darlings. I wish there was something we could do for them."

There has to be, Emily said to herself. But what?

Racking her brain for some brilliant scheme, she gazed absently, one by one, at the three injured children, her eyes resting at last on Ruth's filthy bandage. Well, at least she could do something about *that*.

"Let's go wash Ruth's hand," she said to Maggie, "and teach her how to take care of it."

"Yes, Ruth love," said Maggie. "Show us where you live, and we'll help you put a clean bandage on that hand."

CHAPTER NINETEEN

McLean, Virginia
May 22, 1912

Dear Emily,

I feel like a real bonehead. I don't remember exactly what I said in my last letter, but it must have sounded really mean (sarcastic?). I'm sorry. I guess I was:

1. *Jealous of all your friends and the things you said you were doing. (Your new letter said you don't see your friends as often as you would like. I don't blame you for feeling bad about that.)*
2. *Worried that you were too busy to write to me anymore.*

My life here has been boring. I wanted to get back to America to go to a real school that would give me a chance to see my old friends again and maybe make new ones. I was hoping to play baseball and other games again.

Unfortunately, none of those things has happened. I never leave Grandmother's yard, and most of the time I stay inside the house with no one to talk to but Ginny. Sometimes I help Mattie Lou peel potatoes or set the dinner table. Mattie Lou is nice, and I talk to her a little. I talk to her husband Abraham too. But I sure wish I had friends my own age, even if I didn't see them any oftener than you see yours.

Anyhow, I look forward to your letters and hope you'll keep writing to me. Please forgive me for what I said in my last letter to you.

I'm sorry the ticket seller wouldn't let you go to Washington, because I'm sure you would have told those Senators important things they should know. I'm writing to them, though. So far I've written to seven Senators about the shortage of lifeboats, how there was no safety drill for passengers, and the locked gates in the steerage section of the ship. Only two of the Senators answered, and their letters didn't say much more than "Thank you for writing." But I'm going to keep on with my project until every Senator in Washington has heard from me. Maybe I'll write to every U.S. Representative too.

I do think your mother is right, though, when she suggests that you keep busy trying to help people who are still alive. Something I read last week may give you some ideas for things you can do to help Ruth Weinstein.

When Ginny sleeps (not as much as she did when she

was first sick), I read a lot. Last week I read an article about Mary Harris Jones, sometimes called "Mother" Jones. Like your friend Maggie, she was born in Ireland, but her family was forced to leave the country when her father rebelled against British rule.

After she became a widow, Mother Jones supported herself by sewing. In Philadelphia she met lots of children whose fingers were missing because they were injured in clothing factories (like Ruth). She decided to call attention to all those children who couldn't work any longer.

Mother Jones did lots of things that were very creative and also brave. I'm enclosing the article I read about her. Maybe it will give you some ideas about things you can do to help people like Ruth.

Your friend,
Albert Trask

P.S. I'd like to hear about Louise Kezerian's party if you still want to tell me.

CHAPTER TWENTY

Baltimore, Maryland
May 25, 1912

Dear Albert,

I was so thrilled to get your letter and know that you're not mad at me anymore. Thanks for writing, and thanks for the article about Mother Jones. I haven't read it yet, but I will just as soon as I ask you something <u>very</u> important. Here goes:

Will you go to Louise Kezerian's birthday party with me?

I don't think Louise will care if I tell you about it now, because she made the announcement this week in school.

It's a boy-girl party. I've never been to one before, have you? In fact, I've never been to any birthday parties except the ones for people in our family. (Mama has always made birthday cakes for us, even when we lived in Ceylon.) Everyone in our class is invited to go to Louise's party and bring a partner. I'm hoping you will be mine.

The party will be at Gwynn Oak Park, a beautiful resort (so I've been told) not too far from where we live in Baltimore. The party will start at 2 P.M. on Saturday, June 8. There are lots of rides at the resort, including a goat cart and even a roller coaster that we can go on as often as we want to, and it's all _free_! The only thing I don't want to do is go on one of the boats. After spending that horrible night in a "Titanic" lifeboat, even thinking about a rowboat ride sends chills down my back.

There will be a catered dinner in the evening. Then we're going to dance (waltzes, fox-trots, polkas) to a real orchestra. Maybe you've never tried dancing, but I can teach you a little about waltzing if you want to learn. You may not want to dance so soon after your mother's death. I'll understand if you feel that way.

I hope you can come, because I'm really anxious to see and talk to you again. Also, I'll be in a "desperate pickle" (as Maggie would say) if you can't make it. Louise already announced to the entire class that I was going to ask a boy in Virginia that I met on the "Titanic." (Imagine!) That would have been very embarrassing if you were still mad at me, so I'm glad you're not.

Another reason I'll be in a desperate pickle if you can't come is because of a boy named Royal Ludlow. He thinks I should ask him but I don't want to. I don't like him, even if he is a wonderful dancer (probably the best dancer in the whole school). Louise likes him, though, so I think they should go to the party together, don't you?

Please come to Baltimore as early as you can on June 8. I'm sure Mama and Sarah and Robert would like to see you too. I'll meet you at the train station and show you where we live. Then you and I can ride the trolley together to Gwynn Oak Park.

Other news: Maggie Flanagan quit her job hand-sewing buttonholes at that horrid sweatshop I told you about in my last letter. Our landlady, Mrs. Lieberman, is going to try to get her a job at a better garment factory. Keep your fingers crossed!

Maggie and I took Sarah and Robert to see how Ruth is getting along. I'd been so worried about her! We earned money for the trolley by scrubbing the front steps at Brewer House. (Ladies in Baltimore are ashamed to let their neighbors see dirty front steps. Isn't that silly?)

Ruth was playing with two other children with horrible hand injuries from trying to operate difficult equipment, and seeing the three of them made me want to lock up every stupid factory owner for a million years. Ruth's bandage was as dirty as a rat's nest. No one had told her the importance of keeping her wound clean and dressing it regularly. Mrs. Weinstein was supposed to be watching Ruth and the other children, but she is too sick (tuberculosis, I'm guessing) to get out of bed long enough to know if it's summer or winter. It would tear your heart out to see the conditions some people live in.

I'm sure I told you that Sarah is out of quarantine now. I hope Ginny is getting better so that you can do more things outdoors with her now too.

Don't you get scarlet fever or anything else before June 8, because I won't ask anyone else to Louise's party, especially not that horrid Royal Ludlow. (Besides, Louise would kill me if I tried.)

You didn't tell me if you still like to draw. I wish you'd send me some of your sketches.

Sincerely,
Emily

P.S. I just finished reading the wonderful article you sent about Mother Jones. Thank you! Thank you! Thank you! I'm taking it over to Brewer House right now to show Maggie.

Chapter Twenty-one

"Hush, now," Emily whispered to Robert as she took his hand. "And tiptoe when we reach the top of the stairs."

"How come?" asked Robert.

"You don't want to disturb Mama's class, do you?" said Emily. "Mama is teaching Brewer House's first class in nutrition today, and she wants it to be a success so all the ladies will come back again next Saturday and bring their friends too."

"What's 'trition?" said Robert.

Sarah sneered at her little brother. "Cooking. She's teaching them how to cook, isn't she, Emily?"

Unwilling to take time for a better definition, Emily merely nodded. "Yes." She turned back to Robert. "So if you're very quiet when we pass the first door, I'll take you to the nursery down the hall where Cousin Lucretia's friend is playing blocks with the children. You want to play blocks, don't you?"

Robert made a face. "No. I want to cook."

"Someday you can cook, but today you need to go to the nursery with Miss Folkerson and the children. They have nice blocks in that room. A great big box full."

"We have blocks at home," said Sarah. "I want to cook too."

"Oh no, Sarah. Miss Folkerson needs you to help her. She's never had any children of her own, and she was worried about volunteering in the nursery. But you help Robert make all sorts of things with blocks. You're such a wonderful big sister that Mama and I know you can help Miss Folkerson with the little children."

That wasn't exactly what Mama had said. Since Emily didn't have to go to school on Saturday, Mama had volunteered *her* services to help in the nursery today, not Sarah's. If Mama knew that Emily was here at Brewer House now, she would expect her to go straight to the room where Miss Folkerson was undoubtedly wringing her thin hands as she tried to figure out what to do with a room full of children and blocks.

Emily, however, had more important things on her mind. She sneaked her little sister and brother past Mama's classroom, deposited them in the nursery, and tiptoed farther down the hall to the reading room, where Cousin Lucretia, whom she had encountered downstairs, had promised she would find Maggie.

Sure enough, Maggie was perched on a tall ladder, dusting some books with a dirty rag and arranging them on the top two shelves of an oak bookcase.

"Oh, Maggie!" Emily cried. "This is the most exciting

article Albert sent me. You've got to climb down and read it!"

"Well now, I've got me a whole room full of books here I should be reading, to hear Miz Lucretia tell it." Maggie paused in her dusting a minute and cocked her head to one side as she studied the bookcase. "Which shelf do you think looks better? The one with the books arranged by size or the one arranged by color?"

"It's about this amazing woman named Mother Jones, who came to this country from County Cork, Ireland, just as you did."

"I rather like them by color, don't you? Or maybe I could do a combination of both. First the little red books on the left, then bigger red ones, then—"

"Listen to this." Emily plunked herself down in a worn, needlepoint chair and began reading aloud. *"Mary Harris Jones, a feisty white-haired woman now in her eighties, has probably done more to help to protect exploited workers from the tyranny of unscrupulous employers than anyone else in America."*

"Miz Lucretia suggested I arrange the books alphabetically by the last names, but that takes a long time for someone like me who never studied her letters too much. Besides, I didn't think they looked very pretty that way. What do you think?"

"Maggie!" wailed Emily. "You're not listening to me! Come sit down here and pay attention. This is important."

"What I'm doing is the most important job in the world, to hear Miz Lucretia tell it. She wants all these millions of old books her friends have donated to Brewer

House dusted and put on the shelves so the Reading Room will be ready for folks who want to use it on Monday."

"Well, listen to me while you work, then," Emily said, and resumed reading aloud. *"Known for her courage and electrifying oratory, Mother Jones, as she is called, has risked jail, deportation to other states, and even threats on her life in fighting for shorter hours and better pay for workers in the mining, streetcar, garment, and steel industries."*

Perched high on the ladder, Maggie wiped her forehead with the back of her hand. "I wouldn't be afraid to spend a bit of time in jail if I thought it would do any good for the likes of Ruth Weinstein. Did this Mother Jones ever fret herself silly over poor little tykes who lost their fingers working for old lickpennies like Otto Meyer?"

"Yes! She did. That's what I came to talk to you about. I thought we might want to try a couple of the things she did."

For the first time, Maggie seemed interested. She set her dust cloth on the top rung of the ladder and climbed down the steps. "Like what?"

Emily scanned the magazine article. "Well, the story about the textile workers in Philadelphia is the one you'd be most interested in. Oh, here it is." Emily once more read aloud. *"Of the 100,000 workers from six mills who went on strike, 16,000 were children. At union headquarters, Mother Jones saw children under the age of twelve with missing fingers or hands and was determined to get newspaper publicity for them. She first staged a rally before the Philadelphia City Hall, at which she gave an impassioned speech about employers who flouted child labor laws and parents driven to perjure themselves in order to feed their families. She then planned a march with the injured children and adult sympathizers 123 miles to President Theodore Roosevelt's summer home in Oyster Bay, New York. At public rallies along the route, she collected donations for food and medical help for the children."* Emily put down the article to take a deep breath.

"Go on. What did President Roosevelt say?"

"Nothing. He refused to meet with her."

Maggie's eyes widened. "You don't mean—"

Emily nodded.

"The old blockhead!"

"The march wasn't a complete waste, though," Emily argued. "Lots of other people saw what can happen to children when the laws aren't strictly enforced. I've been thinking we need to stage some kind of demonstration with Ruth and her friends."

"You mean we should walk all the way to Oyster Bay, New York—wherever that is—with Ruth and Nathan and Esther?"

"No, but we could take them to a newspaper office in downtown Baltimore. At one of her other rallies Mother Jones staged a demonstration with women—the wives of striking miners—by having them yell and bang on pots and pans outside the entrance to the mine. I was thinking we could do something like that in front of the office of *The Baltimore Sun*. If we made enough noise, the reporters might come outside and want to write a story about the children."

Maggie smiled. "Yes! That's a wonderful idea!"

"But we need to find more injured children. Three of them won't be enough to work up much newspaper interest, I'm afraid."

Maggie drew back to consider the problem. "We can't take too many. Where will we get the money we'll need for the trolley fare?"

"Wel-l-l," Emily began. "Cousin Lucretia helped lobby for child labor laws. And she's really angry that they aren't enforced. I was hoping she and some of her friends might offer to drive their automobiles."

"Where were you hoping Cousin Lucretia and her friends might drive their automobiles?" said a deep voice behind the girls.

When Emily and Maggie realized that Papa's cousin had overheard their conversation, they looked at each other sheepishly. But then Emily spoke up and explained her idea.

"Hmmph," said Cousin Lucretia. "That might work. But first I'd like to see some work out of the two of you. Two more boxes of books have just arrived downstairs, and all the donated books need to be dusted and arranged on the shelves in alphabetical order by auth— What have you done, Maggie? These books aren't alphabetical."

"Oh, I didn't think they looked very pretty that way. Besides, I guess I don't know my letters very well, and it took me too long to think about the alphabet and dust at the same time."

"Logic is more important than prettiness when it comes to arranging books. Emily is a good reader, and she's here to help you now. The two of you hurry and get this job finished before dark. You can't work here tomorrow, on Sunday, you know, and we've announced that the Reading Room will be open on Monday. When you're through with the job in here, you can come talk to me again about driving you to the newspaper office next Saturday."

CHAPTER TWENTY-TWO

McLean, Virginia
May 29, 1912

Dear Emily,

I must say you offer very convincing arguments for why I should go to Louise Kezerian's party with you:

1. Louise has already announced to the entire class that you're inviting a boy from Virginia whom you met on the "Titanic."
2. You'll be in such a "desperate pickle" if I turn you down that you'll have to invite a boy who is "probably the best dancer in the whole school."
3. Your hostess will kill you if you invite him.

I certainly don't want to have your blood on my hands, so I guess that means you'll have to settle for a dancing partner who doesn't know a polka from a polka dot. But if *you'll promise to be patient with me, I'll try to learn how to waltz.*

Seriously, I really look forward to the party and thank you for asking me. After being cooped up in this house for six weeks, I think it will be wonderful to see you again. There's just one thing you'll have to agree to. If I'm willing to try to dance with you, you have to get in a rowboat with me. You can't let your worries about those "Titanic" lifeboats cripple you for life.

Even more important is the fact that being in a rowboat together would give us a chance to talk about the "Titanic" without anyone eavesdropping. Like you, I have a lot to get off my chest and need to talk to someone who will understand. Whenever I mention the name of the ship around Grandmother or Virginia, Grandmother runs off to her bedroom and shuts the door, and Virginia starts asking questions I can't answer about why God would let Mother and Father die. (You're the only sensible female I know.)

If your letter had arrived a few days earlier, I'm sure I would have told you I couldn't accept the invitation. For one thing, I didn't want to leave Ginny while she was still quarantined, but that's over now. The doctor came last Wednesday afternoon and officially pronounced her cured of scarlet fever.

For the second thing, I don't think Grandmother would have permitted me to go to Baltimore by myself. But she and I had a heated discussion Wednesday night about Ginny's doll that the doctor had told Grandmother to burn. (He thought it might be infected with scarlet fever germs or something.) I actually stood up to Grandmother and told her that she couldn't destroy the doll, which was the only thing that Ginny still owned after everything else (including her mother!) was lost on the "Titanic."

I think Grandmother was impressed by my argument, but I had to make a compromise of my own. Although I had been hoping to go to a real school with a gymnasium and boys my own age, I agreed to stay at home with Ginny, at least for the next year, and be tutored by Miss Harcher. That's the lady who tutored us in London, and she was a real battle-ax. Sometimes I ground my teeth so hard about things she said to me, I could almost hear them turning into powder. But for some strange reason my weird little sister loves that old goat, and for Ginny's sake, I'm determined to get along with her. Miss Harcher arrives next Friday, so I spend ten minutes every morning practicing my charm in the mirror.

Grandmother knows how I feel, and she respects me for my willingness to help Ginny. That's why she gave me permission to attend the birthday party at Gwynn Oak Park. However, she wants to know Mr. Kezerian's address and the names and addresses of at least two of the chaperones who will be there. Also, she says I can't come home alone on the train after dark and that Abraham will drive her automobile to the park to meet you and me there at ten o'clock. We will escort you home and then drive back to McLean in the Cadillac. I know all that sounds stupid, but I decided not to argue with her.

Important question: By any chance is there a baseball diamond at Gwynn Oak? I've spent the last year wishing I could play some kind of sports with boys (and girls, too, if they are interested) my own age.

You asked me to send you some sketches, but I don't have any that I'm very proud of. I tried to draw a picture of Mother from one of her photographs, but I made her look stiff as a flagpole and at least a hundred years old. I also tried (three times) to draw some pictures of you from memory, but my memory wasn't very flattering. You looked like a witch from <u>Macbeth</u>, in fact all three witches. You'll be happy to know I threw all those attempts away. (What would Royal Ludlow have thought if he had seen them?)

The only other pictures I've drawn lately are some sketches for a swimming pool that Abraham and I are going to build in Grandmother's yard. I'm not sending them because I don't think they would interest you very much.

It just occurred to me that the reason you don't want to get into a rowboat at Gwynn Oak Park may not be because of the "Titanic." Maybe you don't know how to swim. I realized the night the ship sank that everyone should be able to swim. That's why I suggested to Grandmother that we build a swimming pool—so I could teach Ginny. I could teach you, too, if you don't know how. Do you? You could visit with us here after our pool is finished. I'm sure Ginny would like to see you too. Grandmother has lots of room.

I'll write to you again after I have had a chance to check the train schedules from Washington and know what time I'll be arriving in Baltimore on June 8. That's only ten days away. I just crossed off today, May 29, on my calendar. Hurray!

Until June 8—

Sincerely,
Albert

P.S. Was your landlady able to get Maggie Flanagan a job at a better garment factory? I've been keeping my fingers crossed for her.

CHAPTER TWENTY-THREE

"Do you really think I'll get my picture in the newspaper?" Nathan asked the following Saturday. He was sitting in the front of the Packard next to Cousin Lucretia, and Emily could hardly hear him over the chugging of the automobile, plus all the honking and rumbling and *clip-clop*ping of the rest of the Baltimore traffic.

She leaned forward from the rear seat as they passed a horse-drawn milk truck that had stopped at the side of the road. "What did you say?"

"Do you think I'll get my picture in the newspaper?" Nathan repeated.

Maggie giggled. "Well, as if you haven't asked poor old Emily that same question a dozen times in the past hour!"

"But I want to know!" Nathan said.

Sticking out her lower lip, Emily blew a strand of blond hair out of her eyes. She had brushed her hair carefully and tied it back with a big bow before leaving home this morning, but the ribbon had blown off her head several miles ago during the ride in the open automobile. Now she felt grimy and eager to reach their destination. "We all want to know. I'm as nervous as you are. Just remember what I told you. Our purpose is to make a loud noise so the reporters will come out of the building and learn about the injuries that you and Ruth and the others had on your jobs. But this is to be a polite demonstration. We don't want to be rude or get into arguments with anyone."

"But I should be the one what gets a picture in the paper," said Nathan. "I was hurt the worstest, wasn't I?"

"Keep your fingers crossed that the reporters will take pictures of lots of you children," Emily said.

Nathan held up his good right hand to show her that that was what he was doing.

With Ruth squeezed into the backseat between Maggie and Emily, the five occupants of the leading motorcar were tootling (as Maggie called it) along Charles Street toward Sun Square. According to Cousin Lucretia, it was there, at the intersection of Charles and Baltimore streets, that the new headquarters of *The Baltimore Sun* morning and evening newspapers had been constructed in 1906 to replace the famous old Sun Iron Building at Baltimore and South streets, which was destroyed in the big fire of 1904.

Behind the Packard were two other automobiles in the procession, also carrying children maimed in factory accidents. Ruth and Nathan had rounded up five more besides themselves and Esther. Riding with Esther in the second car, a Model T Ford, were two eleven-year-old girls whose hands had been crushed in separate wringer accidents in the same laundry. And bringing up the rear in a Studebaker were two brothers and a third boy who had been severely burned in the same boiler explosion.

Because the three motorcars were all open at the top, the lady drivers had dressed to protect themselves from any dust their car wheels might stir up on the unpaved roads outside the city's downtown area. Atop their heads were broad-brimmed straw hats kept in place with chiffon scarves tied under their chins. And over their dresses were long, loose-fitting coats they referred to as "dusters."

As the three ladies had stood outside Ruth's house waiting for all the children to climb aboard their assigned automobiles, Maggie had punched Emily and whispered, "And what fancy-dress ball do you suppose these elegant ladies are driving us to?"

Emily frowned back, hoping that the ladies hadn't over-heard, but even she had to admit that Cousin Lucretia and her stylish friends looked very different from the factory children, whose clothes were dirty and ragged. But that was all the better, she told herself. The contrast would help the newspaper reporters understand what life was really like for children like these.

"Hey!" Nathan called to Cousin Lucretia. "There's a clock! Is that the right building?"

"Yes, that's it," she replied. "Emily, signal to the other motorcars."

Emily turned around and waved the yellow cloth she was carrying to the Model T occupants behind her. "Now!" she said, hoping that the driver or one of the passengers could read lips. They certainly wouldn't be able to hear her voice.

Apparently they understood, because the girls immediately turned around to signal to the boys in the Studebaker behind. And then the boys started whistling and the girls started screaming as they banged the pots and pans they had brought from home and the ladies sounded their automobile horns.

"Y-E-E-E!" "R-A-A-A-Y!" *CLANG! Clink! OOH-GAH! OOH-GAH!* "Y-E-E-E!" *Clink! CLANG! OOH-GAH! CLANG!* "R-A-A-A-Y!" *Clink! OOH-GAH! OOH-GAH! CLANG! OOH-GAH! CLANG! CLANG!*

Heads of pedestrians turned, horses whinnied, and automobile drivers honked as Cousin Lucretia braked the Packard in front of the wide door of the *Sun* building. Behind her automobile, the drivers of the Model T and the Studebaker braked too. Then, without letting up on their whistling, screaming, and clanging, the children opened the motorcar doors and piled out onto the sidewalk. Cousin Lucretia had warned the other drivers in advance that they probably wouldn't be able to park directly in front of the building and would have to circle the block for other places to leave the vehicles. But Emily had instructed the children to continue their noise until reporters came out from the building to see what was going on.

With the Packard still in the lead, the three automobiles turned the corner, leaving the children to create a commotion without the help of the croaky motorcar horns.

CLANG! CLANG! Clink! Clink!

"Louder!" Emily ordered as she studied the wide door of the *Sun* building for signs of any newspaper reporters coming outside. "Louder!"

"Yes, louder!" Maggie echoed. She pointed to the tall windows above the projecting arch. "We'll give those critters inside something to notice. We'll wake up the whole sleepy lot of those lazybones who call themselves newsmen. *R-A-A-A-A-A-Y!*" she yelled, banging one of Cousin Lucretia's old pans with a large metal spoon. *CLANG! CLANG! CLANG!*

"*Y-E-E-E-E!*" Nathan whistled.

Emily saw a man rush outside through the door, but he didn't look like a newspaper reporter. In his blue uniform he looked more like a policeman, an angry policeman carrying a nightstick.

"Just what do you hoodlums think you're doing disturbing the peace like this?"

"We're waking up all them lazybones inside," Nathan reported. "Y-E-E-E-E!" he whistled again.

"Wake up, you lazy critters!" called another boy. *CLANG! CLANG! CLANG!*

"We'll wake them up, we will!" shouted Maggie. "Let them hear us! R-A-A-A-A-Y!"

The policeman raised his nightstick to take a swing at Maggie's arm, but she saw the blow coming and ducked. Instead, the nightstick landed on Ruth's head, sending her crumpled to the sidewalk.

"Umm," Ruth moaned.

Maggie crouched beside her. "Oh me love, me poor little love. Are you all right?"

"She ain't hurt," Nathan offered. "Head's strong as iron. Like mine."

"Umm," Ruth moaned again.

"Open your eyes, Ruth love," Maggie urged. "Let me see your eyes."

Emily knelt beside Maggie. "What happened? Is she bleeding?"

"Doesn't seem to be," said Maggie. "But it's concussion I'm worried about. Can you hear me, Ruth love?"

"I'm . . . all right." Ruth sat up, rubbing her head with her good left hand.

After a moment Emily and Maggie helped her to her feet. As soon as Ruth was standing, Maggie let go of her and rushed over to the policeman. "You bully! You great big bully! Picking on a little nine-year-old tyke whose poor thumb got chopped off exactly two weeks ago. You're a disgrace, you are. You're a disgrace to the city of Baltimore and the whole United States of America."

Maggie was waving her long-handled spoon in the air so wildly that Emily was afraid it might hit the policeman by accident. She wondered if the penalties in this country for striking an officer were as serious as they were in Ceylon. She knew she should calm her friend, but wasn't sure of the best way to go about it. Before she could do anything, a bright light flashed. A newspaper photographer had somehow materialized and snapped Maggie's picture as she was waving her spoon at the officer.

"You piece of baggage!" the policeman snapped at Maggie. "Disturbing the peace and blocking traffic! And now you're threatening an officer of the law!"

"Hey!" Nathan rushed over to the photographer. "You don't want her picture. She wasn't hurt in a factory like us kids was. I was hurt the worstest. I don't even have a hand no more. See?" He held up his stump. "Aren't you going to take my picture for the newspaper?"

A large crowd had gathered, blocking Emily's view of Maggie and all but the tip of the policeman's hat. She hoped Maggie wasn't still yelling at the officer and that Ruth hadn't been seriously hurt. Somehow Emily hadn't anticipated problems like these when she'd gotten the idea to bring the children to the newspaper office.

"Is that what all this commotion is about?" the reporter asked Nathan. "Children who have been injured working in factories?"

"Yes, siree," said Nathan. "Emily Brewer—there she is, that girl right there—said the things that happened to all us kids at work should be in the newspaper. It was all her idea for us to come here. She hasn't been in this country very long, and she don't like the way things is run here. She promised you'd put my picture in the paper."

"That girl?" asked the reporter, nodding toward Emily.

"Uh-huh," said Nathan.

The camera light flashed again, this time directly at Emily.

"Hey! Aren't you going to take my picture?" complained Nathan.

"In a minute. Tell me about Emily Brewer. Is she a professional agitator? Did people from out of state plan this demonstration?"

Emily shook her head, but the reporter was no longer looking at her.

Nathan shrugged. "How should I know? The only people I know who planned it are Emily and her friend Maggie. Maggie's the one that was cursing out the copper. You took her picture already. When are you going to take mine?"

"Right now. But get another kid to be in the picture with you. Someone else who was injured at work."

"Hey, Esther! Come on over here! This newspaper guy wants to take our picture."

Yes! Emily thought. Her idea was working! The photographer was finally taking pictures of the right people! Happy to leave Nathan and Esther to pose for him and to answer his questions, she elbowed her way back toward the policeman, whom she could still barely see.

By the time she reached the officer, Maggie's hands were cuffed behind her back, and the policeman was holding her roughly by the arm. "All right, you hussy, you come with me."

"No! No!" Ruth wailed. "Don't take her!"

Someone else was elbowing her way through the crowd, someone in a broad-brimmed straw hat held on her head by a black chiffon scarf tied under her chin. Cousin Lucretia.

"What's going on here?" she demanded in her deep voice. "Why, Michael Proctor," she said more pleasantly, "is that you?"

"Well—hell-o, Miss Brewer," he responded with a warmth Emily would not have thought him capable of. "I haven't seen you since my mother's funeral, God rest her soul. Your father was so kind to her those last terrible days of her life."

"Father always loved your mother. He loved all his patients."

"That he did. That he did. A good man. A wonderful doctor. Everyone misses him."

Cousin Lucretia waved a hand toward Maggie's handcuffs. Her former tone of voice seemed to have returned. "What exactly is going on here? You're not arresting my cousin's best friend, Maggie Flanagan?"

"You know this young lady?"

"Of course I know her. I drove her here myself. We want *The Sun* to publish a story about these poor children we brought here."

The policeman studied Maggie's face. "Uh—you mean this girl? What about her?"

"Oh, not Maggie," Cousin Lucretia replied. "The little children. The ones who were injured in factories. See that boy over there? The boy whose face is burned? He and his brother both nearly died when a boiler burst. And little Ruth Weinstein lost her thumb in a garment sweatshop just two weeks ago. It's terrible that factory owners—greedy factory owners—hire children to work for them so they can save a nickel here and there. And then they turn their backs when the children get hurt."

"Yes," Maggie said, looking squarely at the officer. "And you hit poor little Ruth on the head with that big nightstick."

Oh please, Maggie, Emily thought. Please hold your tongue and let Cousin Lucretia handle the policeman. But Maggie went right on talking.

"I know it was me you meant to hit, and that wouldn't have been too terrible, I suppose, being as I was yelling at you and all. But it was poor little Ruth you knocked to the ground. And you didn't even tell her you was sorry."

The policeman seemed tongue-tied. "Well—I didn't mean to hit her. You're right. You were the one I was trying to quiet down. We can't have noise right here in the city like the hullabaloo you and your friends were making."

Cousin Lucretia cleared her throat. "Well, Michael, I hope you didn't handcuff Maggie here because she was standing up for a poor little girl you hit. I would have done that myself if I had been around."

The officer looked from Cousin Lucretia to Maggie, letting out a deep sigh. "Oh. Well. I guess I didn't understand what the riot was all about." He reached for his key to unlock the handcuffs. "I'll let you go this time, Miss, but watch how you treat men of the law in the future."

"Yes, sir," Maggie said obediently, but Emily could only hope that she meant it.

When the officer disappeared through the crowd and was out of hearing, Maggie gave Emily a squeeze. "Miz Lucretia works miracles, she does. I thought that man was going to drag me to jail by me hair."

"But he didn't, did he? Everything is finally turning out right today," Emily replied. "I can hardly wait to read the newspaper tomorrow."

CHAPTER TWENTY-FOUR

$\sim$

𝔗𝔥𝔢 𝔅𝔞𝔩𝔱𝔦𝔪𝔬𝔯𝔢 𝔖𝔲𝔫
Sunday, June 2, 1912

RIOT ERUPTS DOWNTOWN, POLICEMAN INJURED

Baltimore, June 1. Local police broke up a riot staged by political extremists in front of the *Baltimore Sun* building today.

Witnesses said a long parade of motorcars, all driven by people dressed identically in black, stopped in front of the building at ten a.m. After unloading about two dozen occupants, mostly children, the vehicles mysteriously disappeared, according to Hellman C. Bauer, 13243 Lombard Street.

All the rioters were armed with crude weapons, such as household tools, but it was suspected that some of them also carried home-made bombs.

"This city needs better police protection," Mr. Bauer told reporters. "Those radicals are just too dangerous. It's getting so that decent, law-abiding citizens are afraid to even go outside and walk on Baltimore's streets anymore."

At least one of the rioters, identified only as "Maggie," became violent with a policeman who was attempting to break up the demonstration. She was immediately taken into custody and booked at police headquarters.

The exact reason for the protest was not clear. After the adult ringleaders disappeared in their automobiles, the demonstration appeared to be under the supervision of a young woman named Emily Brewer, who has just arrived in this country from abroad. Her association with European or other foreign political groups is currently under investigation.

The demonstrators may have lured seriously maimed children to help with the riot in order to call attention to some radical agenda that the adults are working for. Witnesses claimed that many of the children were disfigured by burns or other injuries.

Two of the injured children were Nathan Schwartz, eleven-year-old son of Mr. and Mrs. Morris Schwartz, and Esther Cohen, seven-year-old daughter of Mr. and Mrs. Irwin Cohen. Nathan's left hand was amputated after he injured it in an accident at the Seaside Fish Cannery. Esther's right hand was mangled in an accident at Kezerian's Fruit and Vegetable Cannery. Baltimore industrialist Joseph L. Kezerian owns both Seaside and Kezerian's.

CHAPTER TWENTY-FIVE

Baltimore, Maryland
June 3, 1912

Dear Albert,

*This is the hardest letter I've ever had to write. As much as
I've dreaded going on a rowboat at Louise Kezerian's birthday
party, that can't compare to what I've been going through for
the last twenty-four hours. I have to give you terrible news,
so here goes.*

*I am no longer invited to attend Louise's birthday party, which
of course means that you aren't invited either. I don't care so
much about the party. The first time I heard about it, I wasn't
interested at all in going. But when I learned that I would be able
to invite you to come too, and that I would have a chance to talk
to you in person, the party sounded wonderful. Now I keep trying
to think of another reason to get you to come to Baltimore, but so
far, I don't have any ideas.*

I guess you're wondering what happened. It's a long story, but I don't know how to tell it without starting from the beginning.

From the very first day at school here in Baltimore, I didn't fit in. I tried, but I was different from everyone else. I looked different in my hand-me-down clothes from Cousin Lucretia, and I didn't care about the things the other girls and boys did (Louise's party, for instance). It was even hard for me to concentrate on my lessons, something I had never had trouble with before, because I always came to school tired. Nightmares would wake me up at night, and then I would toss and turn until morning.

I felt guilty—for surviving the "Titanic." I kept wondering why I was still alive when more important people weren't. I don't mean just important rich people like Colonel Astor. I also mean people like your mother, whose two children would have to grow up as orphans.

Papa used to say, "Things always happen for a reason." But I couldn't see any possible reason why I should be allowed to live when your mother (and 1,500 other people) had to die.

I kept asking Mama to talk to me about how awful I felt, but she told me I would make myself sick if I didn't stop thinking about the ship. She told me I should lose myself in service to others, like minding Sarah and Robert so she could get things ready at Brewer House to help the poor people in the neighborhood.

Even Maggie didn't understand how I felt. She has far more problems than I do, but she managed to smile and sing and try to cheer me up. At least she managed to smile about her own problems. But when Ruth lost her thumb at the factory, Maggie got mad, and so did I. And we got madder still when we went to visit Ruth and learned about other children who had been injured in factory accidents.

Then I read the article about Mother Jones that you sent me. I can't begin to explain the feeling of peace and understanding that passed through me. It was like a vision that the saints describe. I suddenly knew why I had been spared from dying on the "Titanic." It was the same reason that Mother Jones's life had been spared in 1867 when her husband and four children died in the yellow fever epidemic. I hope you won't think I'm crazy, but I knew I had to carry on Mother Jones's crusade to improve the lives of child laborers.

With help from Cousin Lucretia and two of her friends who also have automobiles, Maggie and I rounded up eight children, including Ruth, who had been hurt in factory accidents. We drove them to _The Baltimore Sun_ office and created a disturbance outside the same way Mother Jones once did, by yelling, whistling, and banging old pans. We just wanted to get some publicity in the paper about the terrible conditions in the factories where children work.

A photographer rushed outside and took three pictures that I'm aware of. One of me, one of two of the injured children, and one of Maggie waving a long-handled spoon in the air. I was happy that my picture wasn't printed in the paper, but I felt bad that the children's picture wasn't used, because that was our whole point. The only photograph that was printed was the one of Maggie. But the picture is a little blurry, and the article sounds as if she were holding a weapon and that she used it to hit a policeman. I'm enclosing a copy of the newspaper story, even

*though most of it isn't true. Maggie also wasn't arrested, as the
story says, because Cousin Lucretia knew the policeman. Moral:
<u>Don't believe everything you read in a newspaper!</u>*

*This morning, Louise Kezerian was waiting for me at school.
She'd seen the article in <u>The Baltimore Sun</u>, and so did her
father. He was furious. He told her she would either have to
cancel her birthday party or tell me I couldn't come. (Guess
which she chose to do.) Furthermore, he doesn't want his
daughter "going around with radicals" and is sending her to a
private school next fall.*

*Word spreads fast. By the end of the day, all the girls at school
were pretending they couldn't see me when I walked past. Irene
Clayton, my seatmate, told me flat out that she didn't want to be
seen talking to me for fear that Louise would cancel <u>her</u> party
invitation too. And Royal Ludlow put a note on my desk (he
didn't sign it, but I recognized his writing) that said, "We all wish
you would go away and never come back." At least I won't have
to invite him to the birthday party!*

*But I'm truly sorry I won't be going with you because I'd
really, really like to talk to you. Of all the people in the world,
you, I'm sure, are the one most likely to understand how I feel
right now. Which is—*

> *Embarrassed (about canceling the invitation)*
> *Worried (about disappointing you)*
> *Relieved (that I won't have to get into a rowboat)*
> *Sad (that I won't be able to talk to you, after all)*
> *Lonely (because no one at school likes me)*
> *Misunderstood (by stupid newspaper reporters—and the
> rest of the world)*

Reviled (that's a new word I learned from the article
        about Mother Jones)
Determined (Mother Jones has never given up, and neither
        will I!)

                        Sincerely,
                        Emily

P.S. No, Mrs. Lieberman wasn't able to get Maggie a job with
her brother-in-law. Mr. Bamberger <u>said</u> that he didn't have any
openings right now but would keep Maggie in mind in case
anything turned up. We don't know if we should believe him or
not because Maggie learned, when she applied for work at
another garment factory, that she had been blacklisted.
("Blacklist" is a word I just learned. Employers write down
names of troublemakers and circulate them to one another.) No
one would say exactly that the problem was because of Maggie's
fight with Otto Meyer, but she tried several factories last week,
and someone at the last place told her about the blacklisting.

P.P.S. I don't know if I should be flattered that you tried to draw
some pictures of me or insulted that you thought I looked like the
witches from <u>Macbeth</u>. (All three of them! Ha! Ha!) Won't you
please draw a picture of <u>something</u> and send it to me? Please!

CHAPTER TWENTY-SIX

McLean, Virginia
June 8, 1912

Dear Emily,

Today is the day that you and I should be at Gwynn Oak Park together, and I confess I'm feeling a little bit sorry for myself. If you're feeling the same way, I know how you can cure yourself fast. Go find a brick, or a rock about the same size. Drop the brick on your left foot, then your right, then your left foot again. That's what it would feel like to waltz with your old shipmate, Mr. Two-Left-Feet.

Now—aren't you glad you're doing whatever else it is that you're doing?

Besides being sorry for myself, I'm also feeling:

*Guilty (for sending the article about Mother Jones
that got you into so much trouble)*

Disappointed (that I can't see you today)

*Relieved (that you won't learn what an oaf I am
when I waltz all over your feet)*

*Grateful (that I won't have to sulk in a corner
while you go tripping off with Mr. Twinkle
Toes, a.k.a. "the best dancer in the whole
school")*

*Disgusted (with Louise Kezerian for not sticking up
for you)*

*Awed (by your determination to keep working to
help child laborers, when most people would be
discouraged)*

*Happy (that I can at least send you the enclosed
graph)*

*You asked me to send you a sketch, so I've been working
on the one I'm enclosing as a surprise for you. Only two
of the Senators I wrote to acknowledged my letters.
One response was just a form letter. But the other
was nice enough to send me statistics about the
numbers of people who were rescued from the "Titanic"
versus the ones who died and what areas (classes) of
the ship they were in. I decided that the figures would
be more dramatic if I could put them into the form of a
graph. This really shows how third-class passengers
and crew members were treated in relation to first-class
passengers, doesn't it?*

*I'm going to make more copies of the chart and enclose
them in some of the letters I send from now on to Senators
and Representatives. I wasn't working on it full time, of*

course, but this chart I made for you took a long time, about a week. I'm hoping the copies will go faster because I won't have as much time to draw now that Abraham and I have started digging for the swimming pool.

Miss Penelope Harcher of London, England, who is about to become the live-in tutor for Albert Mason Trask, Jr., and Miss Virginia Caroline Trask, arrived in Washington, D.C., yesterday. Her boat docked in New York on May 30, but she spent a week there with a distant cousin before traveling to Washington by train.

Grandmother didn't think there would be enough room for Miss Harcher's luggage if there were four or five people (including Abraham and Miss Harcher) riding in the Cadillac. So Abraham didn't take anyone but Ginny with him to the train station. (He needed someone with him who would recognize Miss Harcher, and Ginny was the logical choice since Grandmother realized that there would have been civil war if I had gone instead.)

Mattie Lou caught Ginny's excitement, and she spent all day fixing a wonderful meal for our "guest": crab bisque, Virginia ham, corn soufflé, brandied peaches, scalloped tomatoes with artichoke hearts, and lemon tarts. I was so stuffed after dinner that I thought I'd never want to eat another bite of food the rest of my life, but I got up this morning and stuffed myself again on strawberries and cream, hot chocolate, ham biscuits, and baked egg casserole. I guess there's one good thing about having Miss

Harcher here, but I'll probably gain two hundred pounds if she stays very long.

Although the party invitation has been canceled, maybe another opportunity to go to Baltimore will happen this summer. I hope so. You and I have a lot to talk about. Have you asked your mother about coming here to McLean for a visit and swimming? As I told you earlier, I can teach you to swim if you don't know how. The pool won't be finished for a while, of course, but you can straw boss while Abraham and I work.

I get up every morning at six a.m. and eat a fast breakfast so Abraham and I can dig the swimming pool until noon, when the sun gets very hot around here. After living under gray London skies for nearly a year, I had forgotten about how sweaty (pardon the French) Washington, D.C., and Virginia summers can get, but that doesn't mean I want to go back to foggy old England.

Beginning on Monday, I'll have to spend the afternoons studying with Miss Harcher (ugh!), but I'll bet Grandma would let me have some time off from lessons if you would come visit. Please think about it. Will you be having a summer vacation from school? If so, when does it start?

I know you're feeling that no one in your school likes you, but I suspect that isn't really true. If it is, your classmates are either stupid or not worthy of your friendship. Maybe both.

I wish I had some exciting news to tell you, but I don't, so I'll sign off.

Keep fighting the good fight. You're doing important things, and I'm proud to know you.

Sincerely,
Albert

R.M.S. TITANIC VICTIMS
(Data from U.S. Senate Report)

DIED: 1,517 total   **SURVIVED: 706 total**

CREW: 899 total (23 women, 876 men)

- 685/899 = 76 %   214/899 = 24 %
- 3/23 = 13 %   20/23 = 87 %
- 682/876 = 78 %   194/876 = 22 %

THIRD CLASS: 710 total (224 women and children, 486 men)

- 536/710 = 75 %   174/710 = 25 %
- 119/224 = 53 %   105/224 = 47 %
- 417/486 = 86 %   69/486 = 14 %

SECOND CLASS: 285 total (128 women and children, 157 men)

- 166/285 = 58 %   119/285 = 42 %
- 24/128 = 19 %   104/128 = 81 %
- 142/157 = 90 %   15/157 = 10 %

FIRST CLASS: 329 total (156 women and children, 173 men)

- 130/329 = 40 %   199/329 = 60 %
- 11/156 = 7 %   145/156 = 93 %
- 119/173 = 69 %   54/173 = 31 %

KEY

- total
- women and children
- men

TOTAL ABOARD: 2,223
(531 women and children, 1,692 men)

1,517/2,223 total died = 68 %
706/2,223 total survived = 32 %

157/531 women and children died = 30 %
374/531 women and children survived = 70 %

1,360/1,692 men died = 80 %
332/1,692 men survived = 20 %

CHAPTER TWENTY-SEVEN

Mama broke off a piece of last Wednesday's homemade bread and slowly spread it with honey. "We had a wonderful attendance at my nutrition class yesterday," she told Cousin Lucretia. "Eight women."

The family was seated at the heavy walnut dining-room table spread with Cousin Lucretia's heirloom tablecloth that they removed from the matching sideboard each Sunday. Robert had eaten all the cut-up pieces of pot roast and vegetables he cared to and was banging his plate with the back of his spoon.

"Don't do that, Robert," Mama scolded. "If you want any pie for dessert, you'll have to sit at the table like a gentleman until the rest of us are through eating." She turned back again to Cousin Lucretia. "Did your friend Myra feel any more comfortable taking charge of the Brewer House nursery yesterday?"

"I don't know," said Cousin Lucretia. "There were twelve children. That's a lot of energy for one middle-aged lady to run after. She was expecting Emily to stay and help her."

Mama's honeyed bread stopped halfway to her mouth as she gaped at her daughter. "You left early?"

"Um." Emily cleared her throat. "Yes, ma'am."

"How early?"

"Afternoon, sometime. I don't remember exactly."

"Twelve-thirty, Myra said it was," Cousin Lucretia explained.

"Twelve-thirty!" Mama cried. "I promised you'd be there all day. Why did you leave?"

"I—I—"

"Missus Brewer, ma'am," Maggie interrupted, "would I be shaming meself to ask for another small taste of your wonderful pot roast?"

"Of course not, dear." Mama set the uneaten piece of bread back on her plate before picking up the heavy platter and passing it to Maggie. "Help yourself."

"Me own mum is the best cook in County Cork, of course, but I swear on the grave of St. Patrick himself that you're the best in this country."

Emily rolled her eyes, not knowing whether to be grateful to Maggie for trying to change the subject or annoyed at her friend for telling an out-and-out fib. Mama's pot roast was *not* wonderful. It was tasteless and full of gristle. Furthermore, Mama had served it every single Sunday since the family had arrived in Baltimore, and then as mushy leftover stew every day thereafter. Emily knew she should be grateful for having plenty of nourishing food to eat, but she wasn't.

"Why did you leave?" Mama asked again.

"I didn't feel well." It was true. She had felt miserable.

"She cried when she was in the nursery. Then she ran out and didn't come back," Sarah reported.

Tattletale, Emily thought.

"Why didn't you tell me you were sick?" Mama said. "Are you better now?"

"She just wanted to go to the birthday party," said Sarah, "but she wasn't invited."

Maggie drank a big gulp of water, averting her eyes.

Mama accidentally knocked the honey jar but caught it before anything spilled. "Oh, Emily! I forgot about Louise's party!"

"It was yesterday," the tattletale continued.

"Yesterday," Mama repeated softly.

Yes, yesterday, Emily thought. That was the day she should have gone to Louise's party, should have ridden a roller coaster for the first time, should have seen Albert again and talked to him about their recurring nightmares. Instead, she had run home from Brewer House and flopped on her bed to cry.

But it wasn't just yesterday that she had felt miserable. It was every day since her trip to the newspaper office. That had been a failure and had only made the girls at school despise her. They gathered in tight little groups on the playground, whispering just loud enough for her to overhear about how much fun they expected to have at Louise's party.

Now she felt her eyes filling with tears again, but she refused to cry. She refused to do anything that would make anyone feel sorry for her. She sat stiffly at the dinner table covered with the Sunday tablecloth, staring at the chunks of gristle and potatoes and carrots floating in a pool of thin brown gravy on her plate and wondering how she could choke any of that awful stuff down.

Mama reached across the table to stroke Emily's hand. "Eat your dinner, dear. You'll need your strength for your lessons tomorrow."

Tomorrow, Emily thought. What would the girls be whispering about tomorrow? How exciting the party had been? How dreadful it was that they would never be invited to such a magnificent occasion again because Louise had to go to a private school next fall, where there wouldn't be any political extremists like you-know-who?

Emily would have to live through two whole weeks of tomorrows, until school would finally be out for the summer on June twenty-first. And all that time not one of the girls would be friendly to her—or try to be a real friend to Louise either.

"I ate all my meat and vegetables," said Sarah. "Can I have some apple pie now?"

"Me too," said Robert.

"Would you like some pie?" Mama asked Emily.

"No, thank you."

"She can't have any. She didn't eat her vegetables," said Sarah. "Robert neither."

"Did too," said Robert.

"Did not," said Sarah. "Look at all those carrots. One— two—three—"

Without warning there was a sudden pounding on the

front door. It opened a crack. "Yoohoo! Mrs. Brewer! Yoohoo!"

"Mrs. Lieberman?" Mama called back.

"Yes. Can I come in?"

"Of course." Mama rose from her chair, but the landlady had already trotted down the linoleum hallway and was standing under the arch that led to the tiny dining room.

"Mmm," said Mrs. Lieberman with a deep breath. "That smells delicious. Just delicious. Pot roast, is it?"

Emily sighed.

"Yes," said Mama. "I'd love to serve you some."

The landlady fanned the air in front of her face with a chunky hand. She was a short woman, less than five feet tall, with a figure like a rain barrel and hair as silvery as dove's wings. "No, no, thank you. That's not why I came."

"We're having pie too," Sarah said. "It's apple."

"And I'm interrupting," said Mrs. Lieberman. "But I couldn't wait to tell you my news. My sister and her husband, Herman, came over a little bit ago. One of his buttonhole girls didn't show up for work last week, and he's replacing her." She nodded toward Maggie. "You can have her job if you'll show up at Bamberger's tomorrow."

Maggie was on her feet. "Tomorrow? Are you serious?"

"Would I be teasing you about something so important?" Mrs. Lieberman grinned as she handed Maggie a paper. "Here's the address and the name of the lady you report to. You're to be there at seven-thirty, ready to work."

Maggie threw her arms around the landlady. "Thank you, thank you." She turned to look at Mama and Cousin

Lucretia. "Isn't it wonderful? Now I can pay you a bit for me room and board."

"Oh, Maggie!" exclaimed Emily. "Now you can bring your family to America."

"Thank you," Mama told Mrs. Lieberman.

"We're all obliged to you," said Cousin Lucretia warmly.

"Happy to help. Now work hard, Maggie, and make us all proud. *Mazel tov!*"

"I will! Thank you," Maggie repeated.

All the women saw Mrs. Lieberman to the door, but Emily returned to the table and sat down. She was suddenly hungry for Mama's Sunday pot roast.

CHAPTER TWENTY-EIGHT

Baltimore, Maryland
June 12, 1912

Dear Albert,

Thank you for the wonderful graph. Your work is really
professional-looking. I can see why it took you so long to make,
with all the intricate calculations and measurements involved.
Yes, "dramatic" is exactly the right word for how it shows the
difference in the way the rich and poor people were treated on the
ship. How clever it was for you to come up with the idea! I'm sure
it will impress the Senators and Representatives you are writing
to. I just wish I could think of something equally clever to show
how dangerous it is for children to work in factories before they
are old enough to operate equipment safely.

I hung the graph on my bedroom wall to remind me of the best
thing that happened to me on the "Titanic" (meeting you and
your family). It also reminds me of the worst thing that happened

*(the sinking and the unfairness of giving first priority in the
lifeboats to rich people). It makes me want to work even harder
to help poor factory workers, especially children who have to
drudge at dangerous jobs and never get the chance to read or
learn arithmetic at school.*

*Speaking of school, you asked when mine will be out for the
summer. Not until June 21, exactly nine days from now. Until
then I'll just have to keep holding up my chin when schoolmates
ignore or insult me. They gather in noisy little gaggles, close
enough so that they know I can overhear, and then they talk
about how much fun Louise's party was. But sometimes, when
they don't know I'm nearby, they say things I'm not supposed
to hear.*

*Apparently things didn't work out as well as everyone had
hoped. The Kezerians' cook, who was carrying the dinner from
the automobile to a picnic table, tripped on a rock in the path
and dropped Louise's five-layer pink-and-chocolate birthday
cake in the dirt. Then "Twinkle Toes," as you call him, got sick
from too many rides on the roller coaster and lost his picnic all
over Louise's new party dress. The odor was so bad that Louise
told her papa she wanted to go home, which sent most of the
guests directly toward the exit too. Also, they may have been
discouraged by the weather. A thunderstorm started about the
same time.*

*So much for one of the "most exciting birthday parties in the
world."*

*I haven't given up on those waltz lessons I promised, though.
As you suggested, I'm getting my feet in shape for the ordeal by
dropping bricks on them every day. (Ha!)*

You also asked again if I could come to Virginia to visit you. I haven't even mentioned the subject to Mama because I know what her answer would be. She would say it isn't proper for you to invite me. Any invitation would have to come from your grandmother to my mother. And she would also probably insist that Sarah be invited too (to play with Ginny).

Now for my news:

Maggie has a real job. (Hurray!) Herman Bamberger was telling the truth when he said he would hire her as soon as he had an opening for a hand buttonholer. Mrs. Lieberman passed the word along last Sunday, and Maggie reported to the factory on Monday, two days ago. (She had barely finished some new frocks she was making for our family. I'm wearing one of mine right now.)

Maggie says Bamberger's factory is much cleaner than Otto Meyer's sweatshop, and Mr. Bamberger won't hire anyone under 14. (Thank goodness!) But the factory isn't perfect by any means. There are hundreds of sewing machines running all the time, instead of twenty or thirty as there were at Otto Meyer's, and Maggie came home the first day with a splitting headache. Also, the men and women at Bamberger's aren't treated equally. The men belong to a union, which looks out for them. They get paid more than twice as much as the women who do equal or comparable work. And the men work shorter hours, arriving later, leaving earlier, and getting a full hour for lunch.

Maggie was so upset when she learned about those things that she went down to the union hall and tried to join. But the men who were there were rude and insulting, telling her to stop being so pushy or she would never be able to catch a husband. (Imagine!)

Lucky for her, a female organizer (from another state) arrived at the hall just as Maggie was leaving. When she heard Maggie's story, she invited Maggie to a meeting tomorrow night, and I'm planning to go too. Maggie says the unions are the best way to fight all the unjust labor practices, including the greedy owners who employ children. But she's nervous about standing up in public to express her thoughts. She's even afraid to attend the meeting alone (imagine!), so she's asked me to tag along with her.

Thanks again for the wonderful graph. I feel honored that you sent the first one to me, before you made any for the Senators and Representatives. They need to see it more than I do! I just hope that you will keep making lots of graphs and enclosing them in your letters. Now that you have the ratios figured out, I hope that you will be able to draw the next ones much faster.

Sincerely,
Emily

P.S. Brewer House is getting very busy. Three volunteers now alternate with each other to staff a nursery for children of working mothers, including Sarah and Robert. Other volunteers teach classes in hygiene and first aid, and Mama teaches classes in English and nutrition. It's amazing how little some of the immigrant women in the neighborhood know about important things. But they'll soon learn if Cousin Lucretia has anything to say. A well-stocked lending library is high on her list of priorities for the house, and she lobbies constantly with her friends to give us their old volumes. Book donations pour in every day for the reading room upstairs.

*P.P.S. Reading the list of all the good things to eat that Mattie
Lou made for Miss Harcher really made my mouth water. Except
for our meals on the "Titanic," I've never tasted anything as fancy
as corn soufflé or scalloped tomatoes with artichoke hearts, but
they sound wonderful. Mama gets home so late and tired from
Brewer House at night that she doesn't do much cooking. She
bakes homemade bread once a week, but we live mostly on stew
that she makes from the leftover pot roast and vegetables we have
for Sunday dinner. After reading your letter, I was so hungry I
went to the kitchen and made the only thing I know how to cook—
vinegar taffy! I've enclosed a little for you as a thank-you for
the graph.*

CHAPTER TWENTY-NINE

Emily's chair groaned beneath her as she turned around again to see if any more workers had shown up. No. There were still only eighteen women in this musty basement room of the union hall, and that was counting Emily, Maggie, and Elvira Gooch, the union organizer from out of state.

Emily and Maggie had arrived early, well before eight o'clock, and in time to overhear Miss Gooch insisting in her gravelly voice that the women garment workers she had recruited for tonight's meeting should be allowed to meet in the better-ventilated assembly room on the main floor, not downstairs in "Dante's underworld," as she called it.

"Hah!" the man in charge had responded. "You don't need a room that size. You won't get ten people to show up. Women in Baltimore know better than to force their way into union business. Our women here stay in their place. You'll see."

"You'll see yourself!"

Miss Gooch had stormed away from the man so angrily

that she had nearly collided with Maggie and Emily as they entered the building. "Oh, hello, Maggie," she then said in a tone somewhat more amiable than the one she had used with the man. "I see you've brought a friend. Is this the little girl you told me about, the one who was injured in the sweatshop? She looks older than nine. Still too young to be working, though. She should be in school."

"I'm twelve and a half," said Emily, who was perfectly capable of answering for herself and didn't like being referred to as if she couldn't hear or was too stupid to understand the conversation. "And I do go to school."

"Stay there," Miss Gooch replied.

That was it. That was Emily's introduction to the crusty labor organizer. Now Miss Gooch, all two-hundred-plus pounds of her, sat behind a small table in the front of the room, alternately looking at the watch that hung from a gold chain around her neck and studying the entranceway to the room.

Apparently deciding that no more garment workers were going to appear, Miss Gooch stood up at last and called the meeting to order. She was a tall woman, even taller than Cousin Lucretia, with broad shoulders, heavy eyebrows, and hands the size of rump roasts. Except for the watch on its chain, she wore no jewelry or buttons or lacy collars, just a gray dress as interesting as lint and a black straw hat that slumped on her head like a disoriented cat.

"I was hoping there would be more people here tonight, but maybe we'll have a better turnout next Thursday after you all go back to your factories and tell your coworkers the things you learn here this evening. Well, now, I'm sure you all know that men in the garment industry are treated better than women are. And the men who are unionized are treated even better than the men who aren't." Miss Gooch leaned forward, so close to Emily and Maggie sitting in the front row that Emily could see a long black hair growing from the mole on her chin. Her voice grew urgent. "Is it fair that you have to work seventy and eighty hours a week in filthy conditions but don't earn enough to feed your families?"

"No," a few women murmured.

"Is it fair that your family of six is crowded into a row house with one bedroom and no bathroom when your factory owner has two mansions with at least eight bedrooms and six baths in each of them?"

More *no*'s.

"Is it fair that men and women don't get the same pay for the same work?"

Still more *no*'s.

"Good. I'm glad you feel that way," said Miss Gooch. "Tonight I'd like you to share your experiences in the workplace. Stand up and tell us about the conditions you work under—the unfair things that employers do to you." She looked around the room expectantly, but no one stood or raised a hand. "Anyone?"

Miss Gooch pinched her lips together, waiting for someone to respond. Emily turned toward Maggie, hoping her friend would tell the other women how Ruth had lost her thumb in the cutting machine at Otto Meyer's sweatshop, but Maggie wouldn't look up from a bit of thread she was twisting around one finger.

A nervous silence overtook the room as all the women, like Maggie, avoided eye contact with Elvira Gooch for fear of being called on. Time passed. Miss Gooch smiled encouragingly.

At last a haggard-looking woman stood. "Our plant has about two hundred workers, mostly girls. The windows are nailed shut, and summers get so hot, I nearly melt. Yesterday the perspiration rolled down my cheeks, but my mouth was dry as sand. I could hardly wait for lunchtime to get a drink of water from the cooler in the cellar, but it was empty when I finally got there. I told the foreman I'd faint if I didn't get a drink, but he said I'd have to go to the toilet if I wanted any water."

"You at least have a toilet," another woman cried out. "There's a privy behind our building, but the stench is so bad, I don't ever use it."

"It's the gents what stink at our place," the woman next to Emily muttered. "Them and the bosses what favors them."

"Stand up and tell us about it," said Miss Gooch.

The woman looked around, deciding. Snarls of gray hair fell out from a dirty scarf tied over her head. "Umph," she said as she struggled to her feet, then looked around again. "Gents at our place get paid the same every week, no matter what, but us girls are on piecework. We show up early, at sunup almost. But gents don't come till nearly seven. Then they stand around laughing and making off-color jokes with the foreman until the whistle blows. They take a full hour for lunch, too, and turn off their machines even before the night whistle blows at seven. Work only half days on Saturday. Us girls never could do those things, or we wouldn't make enough money to pay the rent."

Several women nodded in agreement as she sat down, but no one else seemed to have anything to say. As the moments ticked by, Emily wondered if Miss Gooch would adjourn the meeting. She hoped not. No one had said anything about parents who let their children work or employers who hired children under fourteen because they provided cheap labor. Wasn't that why she and Maggie had come, to talk about child labor?

Emily leaned over to her friend. "Tell them about Ruth."

Maggie hugged herself. She was visibly shaking. *I can't,* she mouthed through the white circle that had formed around her lips. Emily stared back in amazement. She could scarcely believe that Maggie—lighthearted Maggie, who was always jabbering or singing as they washed the dishes at home—could ever be afraid to speak.

Well, Emily wasn't going to let the time go to waste. She sprang from her chair. "I don't work in a garment factory, and I don't know if I'm supposed to speak, but I want to tell you about this little nine-year-old girl named Ruth Weinstein who—"

Maggie seized her arm. "I'll do it," she mumbled. Rising to her feet, Maggie took a deep breath. "I worked—" she croaked. She cleared her throat and tried again. "I worked with Ruth. At—at Otto Meyer's sweatshop, it was. Ruth's mum is too sick to work—stays in bed all day—so her family sent Ruth out at age seven to clip threads in the sweatshop where her papa is a cutter."

As Maggie continued talking, her voice grew stronger and more confident. "Ruth is a love and bright as the sun, too, but all she's ever known in life is clipping threads. Like me, she never had much of a chance to go to school and better herself with reading and figuring. So she asked me to teach her how to make hand buttonholes, like I do. That would earn her a little more money, anyways. I was willing to teach her because I knew Ruth could learn, even if she's but nine years old."

Maggie's voice wavered again, and she paused to wipe her forehead with the crook of her elbow. "Now there's one big difference between Ruth and me, between Ruth and all of you. Hold up your hands, ladies, all of you. Look at them, like this."

Both of Maggie's hands were in the air, fingers wide apart. She held them there until all the other women had raised theirs too. "We all have good hands with two good thumbs, don't we? Now pretend for a minute that you lose your right thumb." Maggie folded her right thumb down. "Could you still do your factory job without a right thumb? Well, sweet little Ruth Weinstein is missing hers. The sweatshop where we worked didn't try to keep her away from the dangerous cutting machine. And now I can't teach Ruth how to make hand buttonholes. She can't even hold the scissors to clip threads no more."

Maggie put her hands down. She looked around the room, her voice stronger, more determined than Emily had ever heard it before. "If unions will protect little ones like Ruth from losing their thumbs—if unions will see to it that *all* workers are treated fairly—that we all have a bit of daylight every day to spend with our loved ones—that we all get paid enough to keep a roof over our heads and our bellies full—well, I say we should join." Exhausted, she sank to her seat.

The room turned so still that a fly buzzing around Emily's head in fits and starts seemed as loud as a rusty lawn mower.

After a moment, the lady in the front row next to Emily stood up and began clapping. Then Emily stood to clap, too, and soon all the women in the room were on their feet, joining in a hearty standing ovation for Maggie and her speech. "You were wonderful," Emily whispered as the applause continued. "I knew you could do it."

The noise lasted for nearly a minute, until Elvira Gooch banged her table with the heel of a shoe she had removed from one foot.

"Well, ladies, do you see the need for a women's garment workers' union?"

"Yes!" the ladies shouted.

"Again," said Miss Gooch.

"Yes!" they repeated.

Miss Gooch waved both arms in the air, the way Emily's

papa used to when he was conducting the Sunday-school hymns in Ceylon. "Again!"

"*Yes!*"

"Well, I expect to see every one of you back here next time with at least ten people from every garment factory in Baltimore. Now go home and get busy."

CHAPTER THIRTY

Miss Cameron smiled, revealing those big, horsy teeth. "I think I should change the rules of our spelling bee."

It was Monday, just four days before school would adjourn for the summer, and Emily's class was in the midst of a spelling bee. That is, two of Miss Cameron's pupils were still having a spelling bee. All the other boys and girls had been sent to their seats for misspelling their assigned words, but Royal Ludlow and Emily were still on their feet in front of the classroom.

It had amazed Emily to discover that Royal was a good speller. Given the fact that his chief forms of entertainment were bragging and torturing helpless insects, she was surprised that he was smart enough to spell his own name, let alone the word *rudimentary,* which had just sent five classmates back to their desks.

"We seem to have two exceptional spellers here today," Miss Cameron said, "so to conclude this little bee before the recess bell rings, I think I'll ask them to define the words after they spell them. Ready, Royal?"

He shrugged. "Why not?"

"The next word is *tenacity*. Please spell it and then tell us what it means."

Puzzled, Royal screwed up his face. "Tenacity," he repeated. "T-E-N-A-S-S-I— No. T-E-N-N-A-S— No. T-E-N-N-A-S-I-T-Y? Is that right?"

"What do you think?" said Miss Cameron.

Royal grinned sheepishly. "I can't remember what I said."

Sitting in the back row, Clint Webster quipped loudly enough for everyone in the whole room to hear. "'Course not! Royal can't even remember what day it is." The boys on either side of him snickered at Clint's joke, but Emily had long suspected a deep-seated rivalry between Royal and Clint Webster. They were the two best athletes in the room, and Miss Cameron always selected them to be captains of opposing baseball teams whenever it was necessary to choose up sides.

"Well, can you tell me what it means if a person has tenacity?" Miss Cameron asked.

Royal screwed up his face while he thought. "Wel-l-l, I guess someone with tenacity is a good tennis player. Like me."

"You!" yelled Clint. "You can't play tennis! Doug Riley, the littlest kid in Miss Washburn's class, beat you in the city tournament last summer."

"I could have won if I'd wanted to," said Royal. "Anyway, I can hit a baseball harder than that shrimp. Harder than you too. I—"

Miss Cameron scowled. "That's enough, boys."

"You need good footwork to play tennis," Clint taunted. "You stumbled all over yourself before you fell down— smack on your face."

"Liar!"

"Royal!" cried Miss Cameron. "That's no way to—"

"Who's the best dancer in this class?" shouted Royal.

"Dancer!" sneered Clint. "Who cares about dancing?"

"That's enough, I said," Miss Cameron repeated.

Royal's voice drowned out the teacher's. "The girls, that's who! They all want to dance with me. Just ask them. Ask Louise Kezerian. If she hadn't been so crazy to dance with me, she never would have given that party at Gwynn Oak Park."

Louise's face turned the color of cranberry sauce as bedlam broke loose in the room.

Miss Cameron slammed her desk with her ruler. *"Silence!"* she shouted, and the room immediately quieted.

Poor Louise! thought Emily. She tried to send a comforting smile in Louise's direction, but Louise had buried her face in both hands, elbows resting on her front-row desk.

After a moment the teacher spoke more calmly. "Emily, can you spell and define *tenacity*?"

Still rattled by the boys' argument, Emily tried to gather her thoughts.

"Tenacity. T-E-N-A-C-I-T-Y. A person with tenacity has the courage to stick to his convictions and goals even when other people make fun of him. Tenacity is sort of like stubbornness, I guess. I have tenacity about the things I really believe in, like trying to stop factory owners from hiring little children—like the time I created a disturbance at the newspaper office so people would read about children who had been injured—"

Miss Cameron's eyebrows shot up on her forehead, and Emily could have kicked herself. She was sure the teacher had read the newspaper article about the abuses in Mr. Kezerian's factories. Most of the pupils in the room had probably seen it. How could Emily have been so stupid as to bring that subject up, to embarrass Louise not two minutes after Royal had humiliated her?

"You may take your seat, Royal. Emily's spelling and definition are correct," Miss Cameron began, but before she could say more, the bell for recess sounded, and the pupils hurried to line up by the back door of the room.

Once outside, Emily rushed over to Louise. "Oh Louise, I'm sorry for what I said about factory owners. I wasn't thinking. Anyway, I didn't mean your father exactly."

"Sure you did. You're right about child labor. I've even told my father he's breaking the law, but he always says I don't understand business."

"But it was terrible of me to bring that up after Royal had just said what he did. I want you to know I didn't tell him about the reason for your party. Honest."

Louise shrugged. "I guess he figured it out himself. I just wish I'd never had that dumb party. It wasn't any fun at all without you. You're the only friend I've ever had. I'm being sent to private school next year, but no one can stop us from seeing each other this week. Want to walk home with me this afternoon?"

Emily grinned. "Sure I do. Yes!"

"If I promise not to say anything to my father, will you tell me all about your trip to the newspaper office?" asked Louise. "I wish I had your kind of tenacity."

CHAPTER THIRTY-ONE

McLean, Virginia
June 17, 1912

Dear Emily,

Fancy is as fancy does! I'll take delicious any day. Ever since your taffy arrived, I've been gorging like a fool who has never seen food before. What a treat! Thank you!

Is it hot in Baltimore? It's been so hot here that Grandmother didn't want me to dig the swimming pool anymore, so she hired some people from Washington to finish the digging and do all the other work necessary (lining the hole, installing plumbing, etc.).

That means I've had time to make copies of the graph I sent you and write more letters to Senators and Representatives. That job is important, and I'm happy to do it. But making the same graph over and over gets pretty boring after a while, so my life is even more humdrum than I described in my last letter. The only change is that

I've decided Miss Harcher isn't quite the old bat I once thought she was. I wouldn't go so far as to say that I'm actually enjoying my Latin lessons with her, but at least something Father once told me finally makes sense. He said, "Young people tend to judge everyone else by a rigid black-and-white standard. But when you grow up, you'll learn that some people may be smarter and nicer than you give them credit for at first."

Father died before we ever went to England, so he never met Miss Harcher. But I think he was talking about people like her, who mean well in spite of the irritating way they patronize you with clucking noises, sickeningly sweet smiles, and "tender" little pats on the head. Since she's been here, I've learned how she was orphaned at an even younger age than I was but managed to get an education without any financial help from her family. That's pretty remarkable when you think about it, and I have to admire her.

I'm also in awe of all the things she knows—not just Latin and mathematics, but history and literature.

Do you think I might be growing up?

Thanks again for the candy. It's wonderful. I mean, it <u>was</u> wonderful.

You still haven't answered my question, so I'll ask it one final time. DO YOU KNOW HOW TO SWIM OR DON'T YOU?

I don't have anything interesting to tell you, so I'll sign off. Sorry.

Sincerely,
Albert

CHAPTER THIRTY-TWO

McLean, Virginia
June 18, 1912

Dear Mrs. Brewer,

My grandchildren, Albert and Virginia Trask, have told me so much about your family that I feel I know you all. It is their wish that Emily and Sarah be allowed to spend time with us here in our country home, and I am extending this invitation on behalf of all of us.

As you may know, Albert was helping my handyman, Abraham, build a swimming pool here in our yard. After a time, I decided the work was too strenuous, both physically and mentally, for Albert, so I engaged a professional swimming pool contractor from Washington, D.C., to complete the task. His workers are nearly through with the project and expect the pool to be operational by July 1.

I'm hoping that you will allow Emily and Sarah to come

visit us for two weeks beginning the first of July. Our community has a very special Fourth of July celebration that I think they would enjoy.

If you are worried about accidents in the water, I will make certain that Abraham, an excellent swimmer, is on guard at any time the children are in the pool. Albert also swims very well and is eager to teach his little sister and Sarah to swim. (I suspect that Emily is comfortable in the water, but Albert can teach her too, if necessary.)

In addition to the pool, there are many other outdoor activities I think your children would enjoy here. There is a lovely wooded area behind our home where the children can climb and explore. And our next-door neighbor still maintains a stable (I sold all my horses after my husband died five years ago) with several animals that are gentle with inexperienced riders.

I feel certain that a visit from your daughters would provide a healthy diversion for my grandchildren. Immediately after they came to live with me, I was so consumed by my own grief over the death of a second son in less than a year as well as the passing of my daughter-in-law that I failed to give proper attention to Virginia's and Albert's needs. Although Virginia is much happier now that her tutor has arrived, I'm worried that Albert spends too much time brooding. He seems obsessed about the shipwreck, the loss of his mother, and the failure of U.S. Congressmen to respond to the stream of letters he sends to Washington.

I assure you that we have plenty of room for guests—two available bedrooms if your girls prefer to sleep by themselves.

However, Virginia is hoping that you and Sarah will agree to let Sarah share her bed.

If you are amenable to these arrangements, I suggest you send the girls by train to Washington, D.C., and Abraham will pick them up at the station in my motorcar. Just let us know the day and time of their arrival.

Looking forward to hearing from you, I am

Cordially yours,
Elizabeth Trask

CHAPTER THIRTY-THREE

Baltimore, Maryland
June 18, 1912

Dear Albert,

No, I don't think you're growing up—not if you have a temper tantrum just because someone doesn't care to answer every single question you ask. I didn't want to tell you before because I'm embarrassed to have to admit it at nearly age thirteen. But here goes: I don't know how to swim. (Papa had far too many important things to do than take us to the beach.)

Yesterday was a big day for Maggie. In the morning she was able to persuade Herman Bamberger to hire Ruth's father as a cutter. He'll make lots more money than he did at Meyer's sweatshop, enough so that none of his children will have to work. (Hurray!) Last night Maggie was elected president of her union, and she is only fourteen, a year and a half older than I am. (Imagine!)

Here's the most important news of all. After the election was over, Maggie gave a rousing speech about abuses in all the Baltimore garment factories, and the women voted for a strike to take place on Friday, June 21, at Lehman's factory on Pratt Street. That's the last day of school for me, but the class will just be having a party, not lessons, so I'm going to join the strikers instead. Miss Gooch (the labor organizer) warned Maggie about things that can happen at strikes, but I haven't told Mama. She would just worry.

I think Papa would understand if he were still alive, though. His favorite quotation said something like "the only thing necessary for the triumph of evil is for good men to do nothing." So I know what I need to do. If Maggie isn't afraid of policemen and private detectives with nightsticks or spending time in jail, neither am I. Marching with the strikers is the least I can do for her and for all underpaid factory workers, especially women and small children.

Evil exists wherever rich people have special advantages. The graph you sent me points that out as clearly as anything I've ever seen. So marching with the picketers on Friday is one tiny thing I can also do to honor your mother, your uncle, and the hundreds of other people who died on the "Titanic." Don't you agree?

Sincerely,
Emily

CHAPTER THIRTY-FOUR

McLean, Virginia
June 20, 1912

Dear Emily,

NO! NO! NO!
I do not agree that you "need" to join a strike. I can't
believe you would even consider doing something so stupid.
You accuse me of acting like a child and throwing temper
tantrums, but you're the one who should grow up. Don't
you realize how dangerous strikes can be? Didn't you read
that article I sent you about all the things that happened
to Mother Jones?
You already helped my family and all those other
"Titanic" victims by taking care of my six-year-old sister
when the officer wouldn't let me get in the lifeboat with her,
so stop trying to be like those martyrs you were always
reading about on the ship. You'll never help Maggie or Ruth
or anyone else by getting your head bashed in or your ribs

broken. I hope your mother ties you to a chair until you get some sense. That's what I would do if I were in Baltimore.

I'm sure your father would agree with me if he were alive, so I repeat: DON'T JOIN THAT STRIKE! I'd run out of ink if I tried to list all the reasons, but here are a few:

1. You're not even a member of the union.
2. You're only twelve years old. You still have another 50 or 60 years ahead of you to save the world.
3. You could get seriously hurt.
4. You could get arrested.
5. You should spend the last day of school having a party with your classmates.
6. You won't honor my mother or uncle or any "Titanic" victims by being moronic.
7. Your family needs you alive and well.
8. My sister, Ginny, needs you alive and well. She knows Sarah can't come to McLean if you don't bring her. (Grandmother's invitation for you and Sarah to come visit us was mailed two days ago.)
9. I need you alive and well. You're the only person I can talk to about the "Titanic," and I've been looking forward all spring to seeing you again.

I know this letter won't reach you before the scheduled strike tomorrow, but I'm praying that something has happened to delay it or to force you to rethink your hare-brained scheme.

Sincerely,
Albert

CHAPTER THIRTY-FIVE

"You're late," said Elvira Gooch. She was waiting on the corner where she had said she would be. Against her wide hip she was balancing several hand-painted signs whose edges were resting on the ground. Some of them were nailed to wooden planks so they could be held high in the air.

"I'm sorry," Maggie said. "We—"

The labor organizer suddenly realized whom Maggie was with. "What's she doing here?"

Emily decided to ignore the fact that Miss Gooch still spoke about her in the third person, as if she couldn't hear. "I want to help," she said.

The woman's steely eyes seemed to bore right through her. "Why aren't you in school?"

"It's the last day before summer vacation. My class is just holding a party."

"All day?"

In her eagerness to help Maggie and the strikers, Emily hadn't really considered the possibility that the class party might last only an hour or so out of the entire school day. Now, being grilled by this no-nonsense labor organizer, she felt foolish, like a two-year-old who had been caught sneaking jam.

"I don't like parties," Emily said, which wasn't completely true. It also didn't exactly answer the question she had been asked, but it was the best reply she could think of.

"This won't be a party here," Miss Gooch said brusquely. Having made her point, she turned back to Maggie. "I've been waiting for you to help me distribute these signs to the girls. A friend brought them here in an automobile, but they're too heavy for me to carry them all at once."

"I'll help pass them out," said Emily.

"They may be too heavy for you. At least take ones that aren't nailed to planks," said Miss Gooch.

Emily didn't like being treated like an infant any more than she liked being treated like an imbecile. "I can manage," she said.

"Yes, Emily's pretty strong," Maggie agreed. "Let me see what they say." She shuffled through the signs, reading the messages aloud. "THE 12-HOUR DAY IS SLAVERY; ENFORCE CHILD LABOR LAWS; GIVE US DECENT HOURS, DECENT PAY; MEN WORK BUT WOMEN TOIL; EQUAL PAY FOR EQUAL WORK; WAGES, NOT PIECEWORK; WOMEN ARE PEOPLE TOO; OUR CHILDREN ARE HUNGRY. What one would you like to keep for yourself?" she asked Emily.

"I want the one about child labor laws," said Emily, deliberately choosing one on a plank.

Miss Gooch frowned slightly but said nothing.

"All right," said Maggie. "You take that sign and one of

the others for now. Me and Miss Gooch will divvy up the rest."

Emily chose a second sign on a plank to carry for the moment as Maggie spoke to the older woman. "It's a real corker of a crowd. Even better than I had hoped."

Half a block away, outside Lehman's factory, at least five hundred people were milling, so many of them that they had spilled out into the street and were blocking traffic. Horns were honking as drivers urged motorcars and horse-drawn vehicles forward through a sea of hand-painted signs.

Miss Gooch nodded. "It's a good crowd, I suppose. But I can't say as I like the ratio."

"Ratio?" Emily asked.

"Of policemen to strikers. I counted thirty-two night-sticks, and those are just the ones that passed by me here on the corner. I'm sure I didn't see all the detectives and police-men. There must be at least twice that many around."

"Already?" said Maggie.

"Yes, and that's a disturbing ratio for the first day of a strike. Usually there aren't any private detectives around on the first day because the owners haven't had enough advance notice to hire any. I've seen some gangs of young toughs around, too, and they can be even more frightening. Factory owners hire them because they'll work for next to nothing, and they're often meaner than the detectives."

"But there are more women here than men. Lots more," Emily argued.

"I suspect they're not all legitimate workers," said Miss Gooch. "You always see scabs at a strike, though not too many on the first day."

Emily knew about scabs from the article that Albert had sent her about Mother Jones. Scabs were people hired by the owners at the last minute. They showed up at strikes, forcing their way through the picket lines to take away the jobs of legitimate workers.

"How do you suppose so many people found out about the strike?" Maggie wanted to know.

"The girls weren't discreet, obviously," said Miss Gooch. "Some foreman probably overheard them talking and spread the word. Well, we can't waste more time just standing here. Let's go join the marchers."

The three of them picked up signs and headed toward Lehman's, Miss Gooch in the lead. The older woman had been right about the wooden planks, though, Emily realized. The two signs nailed to planks that she was carrying were awkward, and trying to shift them, she fell several yards behind Maggie.

Emily caught her breath as she recognized the face of the scruffy-looking boy standing a few feet ahead of her. In his hand was a large, jagged rock.

"Maggie!" she called, scurrying as fast as she could while toting the heavy signs. "There's Billy, the boy at the train station who stole your satchel. Call a policeman. Don't let him get away."

Suddenly there was pain, a deep, searing pain at the side of her temple. Colored sparks danced inside her closed eyelids.

Then everything went black.

CHAPTER THIRTY-SIX

They were talking about her, Emily knew. Although Mama had stealthily shut the bedroom door behind them, Emily could hear their voices through the plastered walls—Dr. Bonner's low and churning, Mama's anxious and chirpy.

It was Mama's voice that worried her. Mama never showed emotion of any kind, not when Papa had died in Ceylon, not when Robert had caught that strange illness over there that the doctors didn't understand, not even when the *Titanic* was sinking and there wasn't enough room for the four of them on the overcrowded lifeboat, so Emily had scrambled out at the last minute to make room for the others. Papa had always been so passionate about everything—his religious faith, his stories about the martyrs, his beloved Latin poets—that Emily had secretly wondered if Mama's placidity, her inability to experience either pleasure or pain, was a rare and unmentionable human flaw that Emily had been lucky to escape.

Lying as still as the bed itself, Emily focused her eyes on

the V-shaped crack in the ceiling overhead as she strained to overhear more of the conversation than the occasional words that slid under the door or filtered through thick walls: *drowsy, hemorrhaging, forgetful, vomiting, slurred speech, brain damage.*

It was true she had been drowsy the past few days, and even forgetful—she couldn't remember exactly what had happened after she and Maggie had walked to Pratt Street for the strike. Had she been vomiting? She didn't have brain damage, did she?

The conversation was getting fainter. Were Mama and Dr. Bonner walking to the front door? Yes. Emily heard it open and shut, and then her mother's footsteps coming back in Emily's direction. The bedroom door opened.

Mama entered on tentative feet and sat on the edge of Emily's bed, like a cat uncertain whether to relax or pounce. She chewed her upper lip and folded her hands into a tight ball before speaking. "Do you feel well enough to talk to me, dear?"

"Yes, ma'am." Emily sat up.

Mama had dark circles under her eyes, and limp strands of hair were dangling down her cheeks from the bun on top of her head. She wasn't going back to Brewer House with her hair like that, was she? Emily wondered. What day was it? Monday? Mama had stayed at home taking care of Emily for several days, and now she had come home at noon to check on her. Why? Mama had gone to work full-time when Sarah had still had scarlet fever. Emily's injuries must be more serious than scarlet fever.

Mama opened her mouth to speak and then shut it again, squeezing her hands until the knuckles turned yellow. What was she trying to say?

Emily waited, studying Mama's face. She looked old, much older than thirty-three. Emily remembered how much older than Albert's mother she had looked when they had sat side by side on the *Titanic*. Both women were widows in their early thirties. Both had pretty features. But Mama had looked ten years older. It wasn't merely that she wore less expensive clothes or fixed her hair in that tight, unstylish way. She had looked *old*.

And now she looked old again as she sat on the bed, unable to say whatever was on her mind.

"Do I have brain damage?" Emily blurted.

"Brain damage? Goodness, whatever made you say that?"

"You were talking about me with the doctor, weren't you? You said I was sleepy and forgetful and that I'd been vomiting. I heard you. And he said I had brain damage."

The corners of Mama's stern mouth turned to a faint smile. "No, dear. Dr. Bonner said you *didn't* have brain damage and that I'd been overprotecting you. He said you probably— But I'll tell you what the doctor said in a minute. First I have something of my own to say to you." She paused briefly, looking stern again. "Do you remember what your father used to say about the 'teaching moment'?"

"Uh—yes. He said that there's a time when certain lessons are most easily understood. Children—and other people, too, I guess—should be taught things when the lessons will make the most sense."

"Exactly. And I missed my teaching moment with you. You were too ill and I was too consumed with worry to talk to you the day you were injured. But you need to understand that your behavior was not only foolish—you were seriously injured, after all—but also deceitful. You didn't tell me that you planned to march with Maggie's picketers, only that you didn't want to go to school because the class was holding a party."

"But they *did* have a party!"

Mama held up both hands, palms toward Emily. "Let me finish. The party lasted one hour, the last hour of the day. You missed lessons in history, science, arithmetic, and reading."

"Who told you that?"

"Your teacher, Miss Cameron. She came to see me at Brewer House after school because she was worried about where you'd been. She brought some of your papers and some cookies from the party."

"Oh, Mama, I'm sorry if I deceived you. But I really didn't know how long the party would last, and I was afraid you wouldn't let me help the picketers if you knew that's what I wanted to do."

"No, I wouldn't have let you help them, so you can imagine how I felt when Maggie came rushing to Brewer House to tell me that you had been injured at the strike and she had taken you to the hospital in an ambulance."

"I—I don't remember a hospital—"

"Maybe not. That isn't the point. The point is that you were hurt after deliberately doing something you knew you shouldn't. Your papa would be very disappointed in you."

"Oh, no, Mama. I knew Papa would have let me go to the strike if he'd been here. He would have told me I should go."

"Emily! You're wrong!"

"No, I'm not. Papa always said that the only thing necessary for the triumph of evil was for good men to do nothing. He would have wanted me to prevent those horrible factory owners from hiring children to operate dangerous machinery and making people work eighty hours a week in filthy buildings that don't have enough light and—"

"No, Emily! Your papa might have helped Maggie at the strike himself, but he wouldn't have wanted you to do it. He would never, never want his children to put themselves at risk. He would tell you—at least until you're grown—to help other people in safe ways, by volunteering at Brewer House, for instance, in the nursery, or in some of the classes we teach there."

"You just say that because you never feel things as deeply as Papa and I do," Emily insisted. "Remember the lifeboat on the *Titanic*? Remember when the officer said that the boat was too full and would get swamped after it was lowered if someone didn't get off? I knew Papa would get off if he'd been there, so I did instead. But you just sat there."

Mama looked sad now. More sad than Emily had ever seen her.

"You didn't see me try to follow you? I stood up, but the officer grabbed my arm and ordered me to stay on board the lifeboat so I could take care of Sarah and Robert. I was so upset I could hardly breathe when I watched you hurrying back onto the deck to look for another boat. I knew I'd feel miserable and guilty the rest of my life if anything happened to you."

"You? You would feel miserable and guilty?"

"Of course." Mama reached over and squeezed Emily's hand.

Emily swallowed against the lump rising in her throat. "Do—do you ever feel guilty about anything else? About being one of only seven hundred survivors from the ship when more than fifteen hundred people died?"

Mama let go of Emily's hand and smoothed her apron. "I don't like to think about that. I try to stay busy so I can put it out of my mind."

"Don't you ever have bad dreams about the ship?"

"Sometimes, I guess." Mama's eyes were watering too. "I can't control my dreams. But knowing that I'm doing something important keeps my mind occupied in the daytime. I'm proud of you for wanting to do good for other people, but it's not your responsibility at age twelve to put your own safety at risk while you try to right all the wrongs in the world. I want you to grow up happy and well. After losing my husband, I couldn't bear to lose my wonderful daughter too. Promise me that you'll remember how much I need you before you ever do anything that reckless again."

"Ever?"

Mama sighed. "At least not until you're grown, twenty-one. Will you promise me that? I love you too much to lose you."

"Oh, Mama! I love you too!" Emily threw her arms around her mother, and for several minutes they held each other tight.

Mama was the first to break away. "You asked what Doctor Bonner and I were discussing."

Emily had almost forgotten the conversation she had overheard. "Oh. Yes, ma'am."

"I was afraid you weren't well enough to go swimming and horseback riding. You did have a concussion, and he told me to keep an eye on you for a few more days. But if you continue to improve, the doctor assured me, a trip to the country would be good for you. I received an invitation from Albert's grandmother for you and Sarah to visit the Trasks. And there's a letter to you from Albert that just arrived. I didn't open that one, of course."

From her apron pocket she pulled out two letters and handed them to Emily.

CHAPTER THIRTY-SEVEN

McLean, Virginia
June 27, 1912

Dear Emily,

Ginny rushes to the mailbox every day to see if a letter from your mother has arrived yet. Grandmother can't understand why she hasn't received a reply to her invitation. I'm worried sick.

Everyone around here has been making preparations for your arrival. Grandmother stands over the workmen to make sure they finish the swimming pool by July 1. Abraham has washed every window in the house and planted new flowerbeds in the yard. Ginny is collecting old magazines from the neighbors so she and Sarah can cut out paper dolls. Mattie Lou has washed all the guest-room bedding and is planning special menus for you and Sarah. Even Miss Harcher is making notes for "teaching games" she can play with Ginny and Sarah.

*I've tried to figure out a possible reason for your
mother's failure to answer Grandmother's letter. Here are
the things that occurred to me:*

1. *In spite of all the people who told you not to, you joined
   the strike and got hurt.*
2. *You're in jail.*
3. *You're so mad at me for the letter I wrote you last week
   that you never want to see me again, so you destroyed
   Grandmother's invitation before your mother could
   read it.*
4. *There has been a problem at the U.S. Post Office.*

*After stewing and stewing about Number One, I
decided it couldn't possibly be the right explanation,
because even if you were hurt, your mother would write to
tell us that.*

*The same thing is true for Number Two. Besides, no
judge would send a twelve-year-old girl to jail.*

*I've also decided that Number Three couldn't be right.
You've been out of the country for three years and maybe
don't know that interfering with the U.S. mails is a federal
offense, but you're much too well-bred to do a thing like
that.*

*By a process of elimination I've come to the conclusion
that Number Four is the only possible answer and that
we'll be hearing from your mother very soon. I'm keeping
my fingers crossed until then.*

*Although we haven't received a letter from your mother,
I did get one yesterday from a Senator I wrote to about the*

shortage of lifeboats on the "Titanic" and how there was no adequate boat drill. He sent me some excerpts from the Senate subcommittee's final report, dated May 28, 1912. Here's what it says.

Trial Tests Steamship "Titanic"
Many of the crew did not join the ship until a few hours before sailing, and the only drill while the vessel lay at Southampton or on the voyage consisted in lowering two lifeboats on the starboard side into the water, which boats were again hoisted to the boat deck within a half hour. No boat list designating the stations of members of the crew was posted until several days after sailing from Southampton, boatmen being left in ignorance of their proper stations until the following Friday morning.

Boat Davits and Lifeboats of the Steamship "Titanic"
The "Titanic" was fitted with 16 sets of double-acting boat davits of modern type, capable of handling 2 or 3 boats per set of davits. The davits were thus capable of handling 48 boats, where the ship carried but 16 lifeboats and 4 collapsibles, fulfilling all the requirements of the British Board of Trade. The "Titanic" was provided with 14 lifeboats of capacity for 65 persons each, or 910 persons; 2 emergency sea boats, of capacity for 35 persons each, or 70 persons; 4 collapsible boats, of capacity for 49

persons each, or 196 persons. Total lifeboat capacity,
1,176. There was ample life-belt equipment for all.

Summary of Passengers and Survivors
Including the crew, the "Titanic" sailed with
2,223 persons aboard, of whom 1,517 were lost and
706 were saved. It will be noted in this connection
that 60 per cent of the first-class passengers were
saved, 42 per cent of the second-class passengers
were saved, 25 per cent of the third-class passengers
were saved, and 24 per cent of the crew were saved.

I guess you think it was pretty dim-witted of me to
spend more than a month writing letters to tell Senators
and Representatives things they already knew. But I don't
regret the time I spent, because the activity made me feel
useful while I was doing it. So I understand your desire to
help Maggie and the garment workers, even if it wouldn't
be the smartest thing in the world for a twelve-year-old
nonworker to join their strike. I hope you can forgive me for
anything I said in my last letter, because I wrote it out of
concern for your safety (and my desire to see and talk to
you again!).

Even though you may be mad at me for writing that
letter, I hope you can forgive me enough to bring Sarah
here (for Virginia's sake) and to let me apologize in
person to you (for mine). I'm keeping my fingers crossed
that a letter of acceptance from your mother to
Grandmother will arrive very soon.

For now, I'm going to the store with Abraham to buy some fireworks and groceries for a Fourth of July picnic. We're all counting on the fact that you and Sarah will be here to help us celebrate the holiday.

Sincerely,
Albert

CHAPTER THIRTY-EIGHT

WESTERN UNION

BALTIMORE, MARYLAND
JUNE 28, 1912

TO
ELIZABETH TRASK
MCLEAN, VIRGINIA

GIRLS WILL ARRIVE WASHINGTON JULY 1
2:10 PM STOP LETTER FOLLOWS

MARY JANE BREWER

CHAPTER THIRTY-NINE

Baltimore, Maryland
June 28, 1912

Dear Mrs. Trask,

I was afraid this letter wouldn't reach you before Emily and Sarah arrive in Washington on Monday, so I sent you a telegram earlier today. All of us appreciate the gracious invitation you extended to the girls to visit your home in Virginia. Thank you very much.

I apologize for not answering sooner, but I was waiting for the doctor to assure us that Emily would be well enough to participate in the strenuous activities you outlined. She had a little accident a week ago, which put her in bed for a few days. (I'm sure she will tell you all about it in good time.)

I have scheduled the girls to leave here on a train that will arrive at the Washington, D.C., Union Station on July 1 at 2:10 P.M. They hope that Albert and Virginia will come to the station with your handyman so they'll be sure to recognize him.

I trust that my daughters will be courteous and helpful while they are with you. I shall expect them to return on the train that arrives in Baltimore on July 15 at 11:30 A.M.

Thanking you again for your kindness to my girls, I remain

Yours truly,
Mary Jane Brewer

Chapter Forty

"Union Station, Washington, D.C.!" called the conductor as the train screeched and rattled to a crawl.

Emily felt a tingle of excitement. "Sarah, we're in our nation's capital!" she said.

When her sister didn't answer, Emily turned. Sarah had left her seat and was squirming her way up the aisle through a horde of standing passengers, their arms burdened with suitcases, hatboxes, satchels, umbrellas, and all sizes of bundles. The train came to a full stop.

"Sarah! Come back and get your suitcase!"

"You bring it!"

Frowning, Emily stood and retrieved both suitcases from the overhead rack. Borrowing two of Cousin Lucretia's bags for the trip to McLean had been Sarah's idea. Emily had suggested that she and her sister pack their clothes in a single bag to allow for more room in Mrs. Trask's automobile in case Albert insisted on driving to Washington with Abraham and Ginny, as she'd hoped he would. But Sarah had had her mind set on bringing a suitcase of her own. That, of course, was *then*.

Now all the detraining passengers—Sarah was trapped in the middle of them at least fifteen feet ahead of Emily— were slogging up the aisle, through the doorway, and down the thumping metal steps like mud oozing through a too-narrow funnel.

Oh, please let Albert be here, Emily thought. Please.

And then she saw him, standing next to a tall, dark-skinned man who was holding Virginia's hand.

"Sarah!" cried Ginny, breaking away from the man to dart forward.

"Ginny!" cried Sarah, scampering to meet her.

Emily's heart drummed. The tingle of excitement she'd felt earlier was now a full case of the jitters. What if Albert was still mad at her? What if the two of them had nothing to say to each other? What if she had to spend the next two weeks watching Ginny and Sarah have a good time? Weighed down by the suitcases, she walked toward him slowly as Ginny and Sarah whispered together.

"You must be Miss Emily," said the tall gentleman. "I'm Abraham. I'll take those bags for you."

"No!" cried Albert. "I'll take them!" He reached for the suitcases, his hands touching Emily's before she drew them away.

For some reason, Ginny and Sarah dissolved into paroxysms of giggles.

Emily could have strangled them both. "What's so funny?"

"Oh, it's Albert, he—" Ginny began, but she was laughing too hard to finish.

"Their grandmother didn't think there would be enough room in the automobile if Albert came along to meet us," Sarah explained. "But he said he was coming if he had to tie Ginny to a rope and drag her behind the motorcar and make you—" Now it Sarah's turn to fall apart with giggles.

"I said I'd make you sit on my lap," Albert told Emily. "And I meant it too," he added with a wink.

Emily stared at him openmouthed. She knew the remark was a joke, but he didn't seem the least bit embarrassed to have made it or to have Virginia tattle on him. Emily was amazed by how much he had matured in two and a half months.

He even looked different, in more ways than just the handsome tan he must have acquired while digging the swimming pool. He still had those interesting green eyes and the wavy hair she had envied and that wonderful mouth, like his mother's, that turned up at the corners even when he wasn't smiling. But his shoulders seemed broader, and he seemed to have grown taller. (Hadn't she and Albert been exactly the same height when they were on the ship? She was the second-tallest girl in her class at school, but now Albert looked a good inch taller.)

Still, while she watched Virginia and Sarah skipping beside Abraham as they headed toward the automobile, she wasn't certain that *she* had grown mature enough to tolerate two snoopy little girls eavesdropping on everything she and Albert tried to tell each other during the next two weeks. Wasn't the main purpose of the trip for Albert and Emily to have time for serious conversations about the *Titanic*? To share their feelings about what had happened to them?

Albert seemed to have read her thoughts. "In case you're worried that Tweedledee and Tweedledum up there might shadow us all over Grandmother's yard, I know a way to escape them."

"How?"

"Can you climb trees?"

"I don't know. I've never tried. There aren't any trees where we live."

"You're not afraid of heights, are you?"

"No."

"Good. There's a wonderful tree in the backyard where I go when I want to get away from you-know-who. The lowest branch is too high for Ginny to reach, but she's afraid to climb anyway, so she says it isn't ladylike."

"Well, I'm not a lady yet. More of a tomboy, I guess."

Albert just grinned.